"Maybe I should g

She leaned over and took hold of Clancy's arm, staring into his eyes for a long moment. Then her teeth bit the corner of her lip before she said, "And if I asked you to stay?"

The fortune that was still curled in his palm seemed to burn his skin, making him remember exactly what he'd thought those words had meant. Something inside him declared war on the rational part of his brain, which was trying to make itself heard. His body wanted no part of that. All it wanted was one thing. Hollee. On that counter. Naked. As if to prove that point, things were already rising to new heights. Just like his fortune had promised.

"Are you asking me to?"

"I wouldn't have said it if I wasn't." She bit her lip. "Please don't tell me we shouldn't."

Dear Reader,

That first crush—do you remember yours? I remember mine all too well. The heady butterflies…and the terrifying angst. There seemed to be no in between when it came to those shivery emotions.

Hollee Cantrell can vividly recall the moment when Clancy deOliveira caught her eye. And she can also remember the awful moment when he turned his back on her. Since then she's been married and widowed, but she's never quite forgotten Clancy. Ten years later he's back, and his effect on her senses is just as devastating as ever.

Thank you for joining Hollee and Clancy as they go on a journey of second chances, learning about forgiveness as they go. I hope you love reading their story as much as I loved writing it.

Love,

Tina Beckett

A CHRISTMAS KISS WITH HER EX-ARMY DOC

———

TINA BECKETT

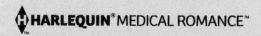

HARLEQUIN® MEDICAL ROMANCE™

Recycling programs
for this product may
not exist in your area.

ISBN-13: 978-1-335-64191-5

A Christmas Kiss with Her Ex-Army Doc

First North American Publication 2019

Copyright © 2019 by Tina Beckett

Printed in U.S.A.

Visit the Author Profile page
at Harlequin.com for more titles.

To my husband, who believed I could.

PROLOGUE

THE FUNERAL MADE her squirm, her grief and tears for her husband having already been spent long ago. The second the news had reached her that Jacob's chopper had been shot down in a remote part of Afghanistan, Hollee Cantrell had instinctively known he hadn't survived. But protocol demanded he be listed as MIA until the helicopter and his body were found.

A year later, both had been.

It was official. She was a widow. The ache in her heart bloomed to life all over again.

She stood on the plush lawn of the cemetery beside her parents as guns fired one blistering shot after another until all she wanted to do was press her hands to her ears and muffle the sound.

Instead she stood frozen in place.

The military salute ended and almost against her will her eyes shifted to a spot to her right.

He was watching her. Again.

When he mouthed, *Are you okay?* her eyes filled with hot tears.

All she could think about was herself, and here was Jacob's best friend—looking as handsome as sin in his dress blues—asking her if she was okay. He'd separated himself from their little band of friends before she and Jacob had started dating, deciding that playing the field was a lot more fun than hanging out with them. So she was surprised to actually see him here. And even more surprised that he cared about how she felt. If only he'd known all those years ago that, given the choice, she would have chosen...

No, it would have changed nothing.

She forced herself to give an imperceptible nod, even though she wasn't okay. Not at all. What she felt was numb.

Her dad put an arm around her shoulder and dropped a kiss on her head, which made her tears come even faster.

Using her fists, she rubbed them away and prayed neither Clancy, his sister nor his mother came over to speak to her after it was all over.

She felt the worst sort of traitor. She'd married Jacob and only a couple of years later had she realized she'd made a mistake. But there'd been no going back, even as the ring on her finger had become a noose she had been desperate to escape. She'd planned on having a long talk about their future once he came off deployment. Only he'd never come home.

And now she was done with love. Done with relationships. Forever.

As soon as she could, she was slipping away. Far away from Virginia. Far away from Jacob's memory. And most of all far away from the man who hadn't wanted her. A man she'd never quite forgotten, no matter how hard she'd tried.

CHAPTER ONE

Five years later...

CLANCY DE OLIVEIRA SETTLED behind his new desk, putting the picture of his significant other on the corner of it with a smile. Gordy might not be human, but he was the only kind of permanent companion Clancy needed or wanted nowadays. The part basset hound had followed him to his car after the funeral, and they'd been together ever since—except for his nine-month stint in Syria. The last one of his career.

It was almost like Jacob had sent the dog to apologize for what he'd done. At least that's what Clancy would like to think. The truth was they'd barely spoken since Jacob had confessed that he was in love with Hollee all those years ago.

Clancy tried to find her after the funeral,

but she'd been long gone. Besides, would he really have told her the truth about what her husband had done while overseas? Probably not. Better to just let the truth be buried with his old friend. The last he'd heard, Hollee had moved away from Arlington, probably needing a fresh start.

Clancy was now a civilian taking his place in a vast network of hospitals and private practices in the area. His plastic surgery skills would morph from treating combat injuries to treating children with facial injuries and defects. The devastation of war had changed him in ways that no one could imagine. In addition to the scars he wore inside, he'd suffered a physical injury, a shard of shrapnel that had sliced a path through his eyebrow and across his cheek, barely missing his left eye. The thin scar had faded somewhat—leaving just a line and a narrow bald patch in his brow. The exterior package had been cleaned up. The interior, however...

He shook himself free of his thoughts and opened his laptop, logging into the hospital's computer network and clicking the different tabs to see what was there. The administrator had told him to take the first week to acquaint himself with the way the hospital did things. There was a staff meeting in fifteen minutes, where he'd meet some of the folks he'd be working with, which included trauma and general reconstruction specialists, and there was a volunteer opportunity he was interested in. He was anxious to get started. Sitting still had never been one of his strong suits.

Which was why he'd decided not to take a vacation after leaving the military. The offer from Arlington Regional Medical Center couldn't have come at a better time.

Prying himself from his chair, he took the elevator to the third floor, where the administrator had said the meeting would be held. Some of the muted but elegant decor made him frown. He took a deep breath and let it hiss back out. It would take time to transition from the sparse military installations he was used to. Arlington Regional believed in focusing as much on atmosphere as it did on quality of care, saying it was all part of the healing process.

And it probably was. He'd just never practiced in a place like this. But at least here he would never have to worry about things like whether their stock of gauze pads would be depleted before the next supply run.

He turned a corner, following the blue stripe on the floor that would take him to the business areas of the hospital. There. People were ducking inside a door to the left, and a couple of others were standing outside the room, talking. Just as he got ready to enter it, one of the people waiting glanced up at him.

Bright green eyes—all-too-familiar eyes— met his, and her soft gasp came as complete recognition dawned. Hell. It couldn't be. She no longer lived here.

But that had been years ago. And she'd been a vet tech back then. So what was she doing here at the hospital? *His* hospital? Dressed in scrubs?

"Hollee?"

The word came out before he could stop it, and the person she'd been chatting with must have decided to get while the getting was good because the woman murmured a goodbye and shot through the door.

Hollee stood there without answering for a minute and memories from the past washed over him. Specifically, the moment when his nineteen-year-old eyes had met hers and he'd thought he'd captured something swirling in those green depths. Intrigued, he'd moved in to take a closer look. Before he'd known what was happening, his lips had brushed over hers.

The light touch had deepened into an actual kiss that had had his hands cupping her face. When they'd finally parted, they'd both stood there staring at each other, and she'd whispered his name. The wonder in her tone had almost transformed a friendship into something else. Almost. Until he'd remembered that she was the apple of her daddy's eye, and Clancy was a motorcycle-riding rebel.

A few days later his best friend had told him he'd asked her to their prom and that she'd said no, but he was hoping she'd change her mind. Clancy had instinctively known that Jacob was right for her in all the ways that Clancy was wrong. So he'd set out to prove that to her. And had succeeded far too well, since she had indeed accompanied Jacob to the prom.

Only what he'd found out about his friend later had made him rethink that decision.

He shook off the thought.

"Clancy, what are you doing…?" Her eyes widened slightly when they passed over his chest, and it took him a minute to realize she wasn't looking at him, rather at his lanyard. Maybe she'd been hoping he was just here to visit someone.

No such luck, sweetheart.

And since she was sporting a matching lanyard and had a stethoscope draped around her neck, she was here on business as well.

His gut tightened. So much for this job being a godsend. "Did you change professions?"

"I did, actually."

His gaze strayed to her left hand. Jacob's ring was gone and no one else's graced it. Dammit. It was none of his business whether or not she was involved with anyone.

More people were entering the room, a few of them sending quizzical glances their way as they passed. "Well, I guess I'd better head in," she said. "I was waiting on someone, but they're evidently running late."

Waiting on someone. A boyfriend? Friend?

His gut gave a painful spasm. She'd already been married once. And Jacob wasn't around to care.

But Clancy was.

Again, none of your business.

"All right. I'll see you in there."

He let her go, purposely waiting a minute or two before moving into the room. That way he wouldn't feel obligated to sit by her. Not that she'd want him to. If anything, she'd made it pretty obvious that seeing him hadn't been a pleasant surprise.

Why would it be? He had done a good job of playing the field. He'd convinced her and everyone else—including himself—that he was not the settling-down type.

He grabbed the first seat he could find, forcing himself not to try to locate her in the group. But of course he did, because what his mind dictated wasn't always followed by his body. She was two rows ahead of him, talking to the person next to her. The same woman she'd stood outside with.

She was a nurse.

Hollee loved animals, so he was surprised by her career change. And dismayed. It was going to be hard to avoid her, and after not seeing her for five years… Well, the memory of their past and that kiss had hit him a lot harder than it should have.

She hadn't changed much, that red hair combined with the tiny freckles that dotted her nose were all still there, and still just as beautiful.

Fortunately, before he could dwell on that thought any further, the hospital administrator went up to the podium and called for everyone's attention.

"Thanks for coming. I'll try to be brief." A few chuckles went up, which Clancy took to mean that brevity wasn't normally the man's forte.

"First of all I'd like you to welcome the hospital's newest addition. Clancy de Oliveira will be joining our reconstructive surgery team. Dr. de Oliveira, could you stand so people can see you?"

He did as he was asked, nodding to those who turned to look. He gave a small smile at the one head that hadn't turned toward him before taking his seat again.

The administrator went on to talk about the terrible tragedy that had befallen several small towns in Appalachia. The poverty-stricken area had suffered flooding from the record rainfall, and just as the waters had begun receding, and they'd been trying to dig out from beneath the mud, a tornado had ripped through, leaving a wide swath of destruction. Dozens were dead, and a big part of the population was in misery. People in the area had opened their homes to those who were without. But there was a lot still to be done.

Arlington Regional would be sending in a team to help with medical care and to get the biggest of the clinics back up and running again. They needed both doctors and nurses to volunteer.

Hollee sat up a little taller.

Was she thinking of going? Damn. He'd already expressed an interest to the administrator. It would be hard to back out now.

"The catch is the team will be gone the first two weeks of December. Close to the Christmas holidays, I know. But that's even more reason to go and help. We'd like to have about ten to twenty people from Arlington Regional participate. A soup kitchen and field clinic are being set up as we speak."

Someone raised his hand. "I'm interested. Where do we sign up?"

"Great, I'm just getting to that. I'm sure there are a lot of questions, and I've prepared a handout with some of the details. I know there's not much prep time, but Arlington Regional is all about quick response, so look at your schedules and decide if you have room in it to participate. If your department needs help with coverage, come see me and we'll take a look at what we can arrange. Lodging will be provided and meals will be served on site."

Clancy could remember mess meals. Despite the desire to be home, Christmas was still celebrated with gusto complete with a holiday meal with all the trimmings. When the meal was over, though, it was back to work. It was after one such meal that they'd come under attack from a missile, and he'd been injured. Several others hadn't been quite so lucky, with five people dying.

He'd been haunted by those deaths long after his wounds had healed.

He shook off the memory and concentrated on the administrator, his thoughts racing. He knew he would be an ideal candidate to participate, since he had nothing on his schedule yet and could keep those surgery dates open. And he was used to less-than-ideal working conditions.

And if Hollee was going...

Since when did his personal issues supersede doing the right thing? They hadn't back when they'd all been friends, and they didn't now.

The information sheets were passed out row by row. Clancy took his and gave the stack to the person beside him with a smiling nod. Then they were dismissed. Glancing over the paper, he worked through the logistics then sensed a person standing nearby. He looked up to make sure he wasn't blocking someone in. Instead, his jaw tightened when he saw Hollee.

"Sorry if I seemed short earlier. Welcome to the hospital," she said. "I didn't know you were back."

He nodded, knowing she was talking about his deployment. "I could say the same of you." He stopped short of admitting to visiting her mom years ago. Besides, Shirley had probably already told her daughter about it.

"I've been back for a while." She hesitated and then touched her left brow. "What happened?"

He wasn't sure what she was talking about for a second then realized with a jolt. She'd noticed his scar. "Wrong place. Wrong time." He didn't actually want to tell her, and he wasn't sure why. If she wanted to think he'd gotten into a bar fight or something, that was fine with him.

He changed the subject, nodding at the page in her hand. "Are you thinking of going to help?"

"I am, why?"

"Just curious." Her voice was reawakening synapses in his brain in a way that he didn't like. Synapses that suddenly couldn't grasp the concept of "in the past."

"With the devastation in that area, I'm sure there are some pregnancies that have been affected. I want to help, if I can."

"Pregnancies?"

"I'm a labor and delivery nurse."

That surprised him. "Do you regret trading being a vet tech for being a nurse?"

"There are always things to regret. But it seemed like the right thing to do."

Her answer could have been taken right out of his own playbook. Hadn't he done what he'd thought was right, only to discover later that he'd set Hollee up for a world of heartache? Luckily, he'd never had to deliver on the ultimatum he'd given Jacob in the months that preceded his friend's death. "Will my going on the trip make things awkward?"

"It'll be no different than working at the hospital together, right?"

Except if Clancy had known she was here, he would have given more thought to accepting the position. Would it have stopped him? He couldn't honestly say for sure. And she didn't know what he'd done back then. Just that he'd turned a cold shoulder to her a few days after that kiss. "True. Only I'll be working on a different floor."

He was still surprised that she was a labor and delivery nurse, although he wasn't sure why. Having children wasn't a prerequisite for working there or anywhere else. But it was a relief to know her face—as beautiful as it was—wouldn't greet him every single day. Because the question that had beaten in his skull for years was: *Had he done the right thing?*

Jacob's confession that he'd asked someone to the prom hadn't been what had shocked him into silence back then. Neither had the fact that his friend had thought he was in love with that person. It had been the who behind the speech. Because it had been Hollee. Their Hollee. *His* Hollee. Only she hadn't been his. One shared kiss did not a relationship make.

Returning to the present, he stood firm, meeting her eyes. "It doesn't matter where either of us works, so don't worry about it. If you're worried about what…happened, don't. It was a long time ago. Before you and Jacob ever got together, and it was obviously a mistake."

At the swift look of pain that flashed through her eyes he went back and tried to soften his words. "Let's just let bygones be bygones." And like his retirement from the military, it was best if he just kept moving forward.

"Thanks for that, Clance."

The shortened version of his name made him clench his jaw. Mainly because hearing it on her lips brought back memories that were better off forgotten.

And if he couldn't forget?

No, he'd grown harder and wiser during his time in the military. And part of that included discipline. The discipline to compartmentalize areas of his life so that they never touched. If he had been able to do it then, he could do it now.

So he forced a smile that was less than sincere and said, "Nothing to thank me for. I've moved on. And obviously you have too."

Up went her chin in that familiar stubborn tilt. Only he wasn't sure why she'd feel the need in this case. He was giving her an out. And himself as well. There was nothing to discuss. Now. Or ever.

"Yes, I have." She moved a hand as if to brush a strand of hair behind her shoulder. Except her hair was pinned up with a clip, exposing the long line of her neck. Nervous gesture? It didn't matter if it was. "Well, anyway, the hospital is very fortunate to have you here. I'm sure I'll see you later."

He was sure she would. Only Clancy was pretty sure he'd rather just avoid her whenever possible. But if they were both going to help in the flood-damaged area, there would be no avoiding anyone. They would be working closer than they'd ever imagined possible.

And he'd imagined all kinds of "closeness"… Once upon a time. His jaw tightened. Why was all this coming up again? Was it the shock of seeing her after all these years?

That had to be it.

As she walked away he was pretty sure it was more than that. And that he was doomed. Doomed to dig up things best left in the past. Doomed to sleepless nights of hearing her whisper his name. But there was one thing he wasn't doomed to do, and that was to dwell on the mistakes of the past.

No matter how difficult that might prove to be.

Hollee punched her pillow for what seemed like the thousandth time and tried to get her racing mind to take a break. God. Why did he have to land at Arlington Regional of all hospitals?

And why did they both have to volunteer for this trip?

She could stay in Arlington, except the thought of pregnant moms not having access to health care wouldn't let her take the coward's way out. If she'd stayed the course with being a vet tech, she wouldn't be in this predicament. She'd loved her old job with a passion, except for one thing. Putting animals to sleep. She'd thought she could get past it with time, but while she had been relieved when an animal's suffering was finally over, it had been the decisions made for financial reasons that had killed her.

She'd gone home in tears one too many times, although she'd known it wasn't the pet owner's fault in many cases. So she'd chosen to retrain, focusing on the human side of health care instead. There were still problems and things she didn't like doing, but at least people could understand what was happening to them and, for the most part, they could have a say in the decision-making.

Adopting one-eyed Tommie was the last act she'd performed as a vet tech. Glaucoma had stolen the dog's right eye, but it hadn't stolen her life. Her elderly owners had turned her over to Hollee, knowing she was the dog's best chance for survival, since glaucoma in one eye could attack the other at a later date, and they weren't equipped to care for a blind dog.

Tommie was getting older herself now, but Hollee loved her fiercely. Two weeks away from her was a long time, but Hollee's mom was going to stay at her house and keep her company while she was gone. And it wasn't like she'd be in another country. Just a different part of Virginia.

Maybe sensing her turmoil, Tommie chose that moment to hop on the bed and nudge her hand before curling up beside her. She smiled. "You know you're not going to get away with that when Mom is here."

She draped her arm over the dog's side and sighed. "But I won't tell her if you don't."

With that, Hollee finally felt a blessed heaviness invade her limbs, and her mind began to shut down. When Clancy's rugged face strayed a little too close, she nestled into her pillow, suddenly too tired to fight it off.

How could one person go from hot to so very cold and indifferent? She'd seen it not only in Clancy, but in Jacob too. A couple years after their marriage, he'd seemed to cool, and all the insecurities she'd felt after Clancy's rejection had returned with a vengeance.

She'd have to work on that problem after she'd gotten some rest.

Maybe then she'd have the strength to throw all the demons of her past away once and for all.

CHAPTER TWO

HOLLEE RACED DOWN the corridor toward the room at the end of the hallway, skidding to a stop when she saw Clancy heading toward the same door. "Clance? What—?"

"It's Ava." His head swiveled toward her, but he didn't stop walking. "She called when I was in the middle of surgery and said she was on her way. Dammit! I can't believe she drove herself in."

Clancy's sister! She'd actually meant to check on her pregnant friend this week, but with how crazy things had been, she hadn't gotten a chance. Of course if she had, maybe she would have known that Clancy was headed to her hospital. As it was, she'd only heard that a woman with pre-term labor was being prepped for an emergency C-section, so she'd come to see if she could help. But she'd never dreamed it would be Ava.

Worried he was about to burst into the room and create a scene, she caught up with him and put a hand on his arm. "Stay here. Let me see what's going on."

His eyes narrowed. "She's my sister."

Which was why she didn't want him charging in there. He was worried. She got it. But that kind of raw, exposed emotion helped no one.

No one knew that better than Hollee.

"Yes, and that's exactly why I should go in first. You don't need to upset her." Or everyone else. Though she left that part unsaid.

At his brusque nod, she slid into the room, and encountered a chaotic scene. Ava was thrashing around on the bed as two nurses and the attending doctor did their best to quiet her.

"You need to hold still!"

"My baby! It's too early!" The fear in that voice was almost Hollee's undoing. But she held it in and went to the nurse who was trying to physically hold Ava down.

"She's a friend. Let me try."

"Okay, but put on a mask, she tested positive for influenza b."

Oh, God. Not good. She took the mask the nurse thrust in her hands and pulled on gloves, then she smoothed Ava's bangs out of the way, not liking the heat that rose in waves from her forehead. The fever explained some of her agitation. "Ava, it's Hollee. Can you look at me?"

"Hollee?" Her demeanor changed almost instantly, and she sagged against the bed. "What's happening?"

She, Clancy, Jacob and Ava had all been so close back in the day. She and Ava were still friends, but Hollee avoided talking about Clancy. And when Ava had made passing comments about where he'd been currently stationed, Hollee had just smiled and nodded, then changed the subject. Her friend hadn't mentioned him leaving the military. Of course, her friend had had other things on her mind.

"The baby's coming." Fresh pain speared through Hollee. What she wouldn't have given to hear those words during her marriage. "You need to let them take you.

They're going to do everything they can for both of you."

Tears streaming down her face, Ava nodded. "She's supposed to be my Christmas Eve baby. Please don't let anything happen to her."

A promise no one could make.

Hollee stepped back to let the other nurse take over again as an anesthesiologist swept in. "What do we have?"

"Preterm labor secondary to flu. We need to get her into the OR. Do you want to do the epidural here or there?"

"There."

One of the worst things that could happen to the maternity ward was for the flu to find its way inside these protected hallways.

As if reading her thoughts, Dr. Latrobe grimaced. "We'll need to follow protocols for disinfecting the ward. I've already called it in."

Hollee needed to let Clancy know what was happening. "Does the baby look okay?"

Latrobe glanced up. "She's five weeks early, but the baby's registering some early signs of distress. The sooner we deliver her the better."

She took that as her clue to get out of their way. She went back to Ava. "I'll check in on you as soon as I know which room you're in. Dr. Latrobe is one of Arlington's finest, so you're in great hands."

"No! Don't leave!"

Fearing Ava was going to start getting agitated again, she said, "Clancy's outside, and he's worried sick. I need to let him know what's going on."

"Poor Clancy." Ava's face flushed with fever. "He had a thing for…" Her face contorted as a contraction hit.

Hollee turned to leave while she could. Peeling off her gloves and mask, she pumped a couple of squirts of hand sanitizer before touching the door. She encountered resistance in pushing it open and found Clancy with one hand on the wooden surface as if he'd gotten tired of waiting.

"You can't go in there. She has the flu. They're taking precautions to keep it from spreading."

"Damn. I asked her to get her flu shot. I thought she did, but maybe not."

Ava had always been the free-spirited, independent one in their group. Even so, she'd been devastated when the baby's father had decided he couldn't do the whole parental responsibility thing. As if to prove that fact, he'd found someone else almost immediately after they'd broken up. "You know about the dad."

He gave her a searching look before nodding. "Yeah, he made her promises he never intended to keep. He should be ashamed."

Had Clancy aimed that jab at himself? They'd shared a kiss that had been pretty hot and heavy, but a week later he'd become someone she hadn't recognized. All he'd said was that the kiss had been a mistake, showing up with another girl soon afterward. And another one a few weeks after that. It had been a slap in the face and had proved that bad boys did not make good marriage material. Even Jacob had commented on the way Clancy had been acting.

While she'd still been stinging from Clancy's rejection, Jacob had asked her out, and she'd accepted. At first it had been a way to get back at him. But slowly, over the course of six months, she'd realized she and Jacob actually had a lot in common and when he'd proposed, she said yes. She'd loved him, but that spark of passion she'd felt for Clancy had never been there.

At first she'd thought it was because she'd over-romanticized that kiss and the connection she thought they'd shared. That feeling had gotten worse when Jacob seemed to distance himself emotionally. Initially, she'd chalked it up to her imagination. But a year before he died, that apathy had become marked, and her request to start a family as a last-ditch attempt to put things right had been met with a chilly response. She'd been crushed, and a seed of inadequacy had sprouted. First Clancy and then Jacob. Was there something about her that drove away people she cared about?

All but Ava. They'd remained close, but she'd never felt comfortable sharing her problems with Clancy or Jacob with her. Clancy was her brother. And Jacob…well, he'd been one of Ava's friends too.

In the end, Clancy hadn't even come to their wedding, something that had hurt both her and Jacob.

The funeral had actually been the first time she'd seen him since getting married.

That had been five years ago. It might as well have been a lifetime.

Ava was whisked out of the room and down the hallway, reminding Hollee what was really important right now—and it certainly wasn't her melancholy thoughts. Or things she could no longer change.

Clancy's face was a tense mask, and she gripped his arm, the warmth of his skin making her realize how cold her own hands had become. Ava had a big team of staff with her, and Clancy had no one right now, and she ached for him. "Come on. Let's grab a cup of coffee. And then we'll sit and wait for news."

"I want to be in there."

"You can't, Clance. You know that. Ava needs to concentrate and so does her team. And the last thing you need is to carry the virus into one of your surgeries."

"Hell, how did I not know she was sick?"

She smiled. "Are you serious? Ava is one of the strongest people I know. She's also the most stubborn. 'Show no weakness'— remember?"

That had always been the de Oliveira siblings' motto.

The flexing of muscles made her realize her fingers were still clutching his upper arm. She released him in a hurry.

"I can't believe she didn't come in sooner." He dragged a hand through his hair.

"I've been checking on her periodically but, honestly, she probably didn't even realize she had the flu. We get sick, and we wait it out. It's the way humans are geared. She had a pretty high fever, which is probably what triggered labor."

He leaned a shoulder again the wall. "She wants this baby. Despite everything."

"Of course she does." Hollee would have too, had the situation been reversed. But it wasn't. She swallowed away the sudden lump in her throat and inclined her head to point down the hallway. "The sooner we hit the cafeteria, the sooner we can come back and wait for news."

"Are you on break?

"I actually worked the night shift. I just got off about fifteen minutes ago, but I heard the noise and decided to see if I could help."

He nodded. "I'm glad you were here. I might have gotten myself tossed out of the hospital before I'd been in town a week."

"That would be unfortunate. Especially with the Appalachia trip coming up."

And why had she even brought up the relief mission? The last thing she needed to be thinking about right now were those two weeks. Not when she hadn't quite figured out how she felt about being there with him.

They made their way to the first floor, and as the elevator doors opened she was met with the hospital's Christmas trimmings that had gone up in the last couple of days. Three festive trees were clustered to the side of the huge glass entry doors, the sparkle of silvery tinsel catching the light. On the other side stood a life-sized animated Santa, his bag of toys thrown over one shoulder, his head swiveling from side to side as if looking for his sleigh.

Above them, glittery snowflakes hung from fishing line, the climate-control system making them dance.

She'd always loved this time of year. "The hospital does a great job decorating."

"Hmm…"

The sound was so noncommittal that it made her laugh. "You don't like it?"

"It's just different from the places I've worked."

Of course it was. "The military doesn't decorate for the holidays?"

"They do, it's just not normally so…" He paused, as if searching for the right word. "So extravagant."

Hollee looked with different eyes and could see how he might think that. "I'm sure where we're going, then, you'll feel right at home." Then, wondering if that sounded pompous, she added, "It's not the decorations that make Christmas special. It's the spirit behind it. Arlington Regional has a lot of children who walk through those doors. And sometimes they need a little bit of hope—a little bit of magic."

"I never thought of it that way. I guess I'm used to dealing with cynical adults whose deep pockets only give up funds for other things."

"Things that save lives." She smiled. "But you're right. I think it all depends on its target audience."

If things went as planned she would be here to help out on at least one of the hospital's "Staff Santa" afternoons in the next couple of weeks, when they handed out gifts in the pediatric ward. It was always fun to see who they got to play the part of Santa. After that, she'd be away in Appalachia, in a town called Bender, for the rest of the festivities, playing a completely different kind of Santa. Two groups so very different but that both needed a shot of hope and happiness.

They arrived in the cafeteria, which was also decorated for the season, boasting small centerpieces on each of the laminate tables. She headed straight for the coffee machine, where she dumped a couple of sealed creamers titled "Mint Fantasy" and three packets of sugar into a cup.

He smiled. "I see you like a little coffee with your flavored syrup."

"It's the only way to enjoy it." She scrunched her nose. "I'll never understand how people can drink theirs black."

"Since that's how I like mine…"

"Okay, so maybe I was being a little judgmental. But for me, coffee is a dessert. Best savored in tiny delicious sips that make you tingle all over. Sweet, luscious and silky smooth." She closed her eyes for a second, her tongue already anticipating the flavor.

Clancy didn't answer, and when she glanced up, she found his eyes on her in a way that made her swallow. Oh, God. She'd made her coffee sound almost like…sex.

Strangely, they'd only shared a single kiss but, like her dessert coffee, she could still taste him. That light touch between them had been romantic and sweet and had hinted at things that had made her skin heat.

Their kiss had happened at Christmas too, and she could still remember exactly what had led up to it. Ava had pointed above her at something on the ceiling of her and Clancy's childhood home with a wink, and when Hollee had glanced up, she'd seen a sprig of mistletoe.

And she had been standing right underneath it. And Clancy… She could still see his mischievous grin. That time he'd kissed her on the cheek. He'd saved the real kiss for later that evening, when he'd driven her home. Only that time he'd been the one holding the sprig. And when their lips had met…

She closed her eyes, suddenly angry with herself for even thinking of that night.

It might have meant something to her, but it hadn't to him. He'd made that very clear.

It was as if someone had flipped a switch and turned Clancy into a totally different person. He'd still been intense, his loose bad-boy vibe deadly to the senses. Obviously a lot of other women had found him just as attractive. He still was.

When his attitude toward her had shifted, she'd nursed that hurt until it had festered, convincing her that Jacob was the better choice. After all, she felt like she knew him, whereas Clancy had become a stranger. When Jacob had wanted to save sex for their wedding day, she'd been fine with it. But when they'd finally slept together, it had been a huge letdown, and she wasn't sure why. But she'd loved Jacob and had convinced herself it didn't matter.

But maybe it had. Maybe if she and Clancy had had let-down sex, she wouldn't be sitting here now wondering if he would have been as delicious as her coffee.

She turned away, feeling like she was betraying Jacob's memory somehow. Maybe she'd been guilty of comparing them all along, and Jacob had figured it out. Maybe that's why he'd changed.

Forget it. She concentrated on pouring

and stirring her coffee and snapping on the lid. She should have just gone home, instead of offering to keep Clancy company. Tearing open old wounds was not something she was interested in doing. Especially if it would cause forgotten memories to come creeping back, dragging a matching bag of emotions with it.

"Ready to head to the waiting room?" she asked.

"Yes." Then he frowned, touching her hand. "Thank you for checking on Ava. And being her friend."

"She's always been there when I've needed her. How could I do any less?"

"Well, I'm glad you were there anyway."

"I'm sorry about the father. It was a rough time for her."

He shrugged. "Mom didn't even tell me what happened until I came home. I knew she was expecting, but not that he'd run off with someone else while I was still in Afghanistan. Maybe that was a good thing."

"Will you go back overseas?"

"No. I was ready for a change."

Something shifted in his demeanor, making her say, "It couldn't have been easy." Her glance went back to his face and the separation in his eyebrow. If anything, the scar made him look even more gorgeous, which was ridiculous. A scar was simply epithelial tissue that filled in a wound. It didn't change who he was.

Or did it? He seemed less carefree than he had ten years ago. Harder in ways she couldn't quite put her finger on. He was twenty-nine, just two years older than she was. There were no strands of gray in that thick, dark head of hair, but he almost seemed ancient, his frown line carving a deep groove that nothing would erase. She hated to think what he'd seen over there.

As they walked back toward the elevators, Neil Vickers, the hospital administrator, stopped them. "I don't know if either of you have been in the staff lounge, but I put a sign-up sheet in there. I want to get an idea of how many we have for the Bender trip." He looked from one to the other. "That is if you two are still interested in going."

Hollee didn't hesitate. "I am. I'll make sure I put my name on the list."

"Great. FEMA has just finished setting

up a disaster relief camp. So they should be ready for us by the time our group arrives."

Clancy hadn't said anything, and she wondered if he'd changed his mind about going. Neil must have thought along the same lines because he glanced over at him. "How are you settling in?"

"So far, so good. I'll take a look at the sign-up sheet."

Hmm, that was rather noncommittal. What happened to all that talk about them both being adults and able to handle situations like this?

If he decided not to go, that would be a relief, right?

"That's all I can ask," Neil said.

"My sister is in surgery right now for preterm labor, and my decision has to hinge on the outcome."

The administrator frowned. "I didn't know. I'm sorry."

"Not a problem. Hopefully everything will turn out all right, and I can join the team."

Hollee had almost forgotten about that. Of course he wanted to see what happened with Ava and the baby. She felt like a fool for thinking his hesitation had anything to do with her.

She steered the conversation away from the subject, hoping to reassure Clancy that everything would turn out okay. "Do you think it would be all right if I bring some Christmas lights to decorate the tents or wherever we end up staying?"

"I didn't see anything against that in the paperwork. It might even help morale. We've already planned on bringing some small gifts for the kids. They're going to send me a rough count of the numbers once they get organized."

"That's great."

"Don't forget to sign up," he said again, before waving and heading the way they'd just come. Why not? Even Neil had to eat.

"Let's head right to Maternity," she said. "I can sign up afterward."

"Are you sure?"

"Yes, I'm anxious to see if there's any word."

Making their way there, they stopped at the nurses' station, and the person behind the desk gave them a smile, not even asking what they wanted. "She's doing well. The baby's out and being assessed. She's tiny, but perfect. I don't think she's going to need as much support as many born that early."

Clancy planted a hand on the desk as if to support himself. "Can we see her?"

"Not yet. They're still closing her up." The nurse hesitated. "And she does have the flu, so we're taking extra precautions."

"We've all had the flu shot, obviously, but we'll be careful."

Wow, Clancy had said "we" as if expecting her to go with him to see Ava. And of course she wanted to. Even if seeing the relief in his eyes had just about done her in. How hard would it be to see Clancy's niece, knowing that his family was growing, while she was alone?

In five years of marriage, Jacob had continually put off having children, at first saying they had plenty of time. The last time, he'd said he wasn't sure if he wanted children at all…with her.

Those words had hurt in a way that went beyond description. But he'd said he didn't want a divorce, he wanted to work things out, even though she'd seen no evidence of that before his last deployment.

In the end, nothing had been settled between them. Had Jacob somehow known about her youthful crush on Clancy? No. Of course not. That had been over before they'd gotten married. And Hollee never would have cheated on him. Not even with Clancy. Her infatuation had been just the foolish stuff of youth.

She was over it now. And she'd donned her anti-Clancy armor as soon as she'd seen him again. She was well protected and ready for anything.

At least, she hoped she was. Especially if he ended up going on the relief trip. The last thing she needed to do was dig up that old crush and start mooning over the man again. Especially if he still played the field, like he had when they'd been younger. If that was the case, and he tempted her to share more than a simple kiss, she would be setting herself up for a whole lot of hurt. And this time there would be no one there to catch her when she fell.

CHAPTER THREE

CLANCY PUT HIS gloved hand through the opening of the incubator and touched Jennifer Jay de Oliveira's tiny hand, marveling at the sweet face. The Jay stood for Jacob, a nod to their friend. That rankled. When he got the chance he was going to advise Ava to choose something else. But he didn't want to do that in front of Hollee.

He didn't want to hurt her if he didn't have to. If that meant taking his old friend's secret to the grave and letting her continue to think Clancy had been a jerk back then, so be it. If he hadn't been such a kid at the time, he might have sat back and thought for a while before letting his friend's veiled hints and his own insecurities convince him that he was not what Hollee—who was valedictorian of her class—needed. What she deserved. But at the time he'd thought Jacob was right.

Clancy had coasted along for most of high school, wandering aimlessly, drifting from one pretty girl to another. His friends had been the one constant in his life. Until he'd kissed Hollee and found it mattered more than he had expected it to. And then even that friendship had been destroyed. Thanks to his own stupidity.

His life had changed when he'd joined the military and had seen the need for medical personnel. It was like he'd found his purpose in life.

"She's so beautiful." The low voice of the person he'd just been ruminating about slid past his ear, making his insides tighten.

"Yes, she is." He'd invited her here. He wasn't sure why, except that Ava and Hollee were close friends, their friendship bound so tightly together that they'd weathered all the ups and downs of childhood. Not so with his and Hollee's friendship. He'd made a choice he'd never dreamed he'd regret.

But he did regret it, even though Hollee had been happy with Jacob, and since she'd never learned the truth, she continued to believe her marriage had been perfect.

Clancy had done his damnedest to stay busy, dating lots of women. He hadn't wanted Jacob or Hollee to guess the battle going on inside him, so he'd played up the freewheeling commitment-phobe aspect of his personality.

Maybe there'd been more to the act than he realized, since he was still single and had no desire to change that fact.

"At least Ava is okay, even though she can't see Jennifer yet."

They'd come to see the baby first to avoid any possibility that they'd pass something from mom to newborn. As it was, Ava wouldn't be able to see her baby for four or five days, until the period of contagion was over. It was for the baby's safety mostly, but Ava had been through an ordeal on top of being sick. She needed rest, and her body needed time to heal. She could still provide nourishment for the infant, since the flu virus didn't pass into breast milk. She couldn't feed her directly, but she could pump and have it sent to the NICU.

He turned and glanced at Hollee, noticing

that she had a faraway look in her eye. She and Jacob had never had kids. Was she regretting that? He hadn't talked to his friend enough after his engagement to know if there was a reason, other than a choice he and Hollee had made. Maybe they couldn't have kids. Or maybe he hadn't wanted to be tied down by them.

That would explain a lot, actually, knowing what he did about Jacob.

"Better to wait and be sure than to endanger the baby out of impatience."

He'd have done well to heed that advice himself.

"Yes, I agree."

"Do you want to touch her?" he asked.

"Oh…um, I'm good. You take all the time you need."

A shakiness to her voice made him pause. "You don't like cuddling babies?"

"I do. My mom is watching mine."

Shock made him turn around, his hands sliding out of the incubator's access ports. "Excuse me?" She had a child? He'd assumed…

"Well, maybe I should amend that. My 'baby' has four legs and is covered with fur."

He went slack with a relief that took him by surprise. "A dog?"

"A German shepherd named Tommie."

"I actually have a dog too. Only he's a basset hound mix."

She laughed. "I love bassets."

"He's quite a character. Mom comes over to let him out during the day. She's coming up to see Ava and the baby in a little while."

"I'd love to meet your dog sometime."

A sliver of surprise went through him. She'd barely said twenty words since they'd come into the NICU area, and the change from then until now was dramatic. Her eyes were bright green and a smile revealed a peek-a-boo dimple at the corner of her mouth that he'd almost forgotten existed. It fascinated him as much now as it had when they had been teenagers. It was what had drawn his gaze repeatedly to her mouth after that kiss on the cheek, and the very thing that had instigated the very real kiss at her house later that night.

Dragging his gaze away, he focused on her eyes instead. "We'll have to get them together for a walk, although I have to warn you that Gordy doesn't always match his soulful brown eyes. Sometimes he can be a grump."

"That's okay. Tommie has enough cheer for five dogs."

What the hell was he doing? They were not two single parents planning play dates. Seeing her outside the hospital was not a good idea. But since they might be spending two weeks together in the near future, this might be a good opportunity to ease their way into things. It wasn't like they were going on an actual date. Just walking their dogs together.

"I guess we'll see. It looks like Ava and the baby will be okay, and if that's the case I'll probably go down to the Appalachian area with everyone else. What are you doing with your dog while you're gone?"

"The same as what you're doing while you're at work. My mom will come over and take care of her. She'll probably stay at the house with her, actually. She has a soft spot for Tommie. It almost makes me jealous at times."

He stiffened. That had been exactly what had gotten him into trouble with Hollee. He'd had a soft spot for her that had morphed into something else entirely. And, hell, if he hadn't been a jealous bastard the day of her wedding, even though he'd been a continent away. He'd drunk himself into oblivion just to keep from calling Jacob and saying he'd changed his mind. That the union no longer had his blessing.

Knowing what he did now, maybe it would have been better if he had. But hindsight was twenty-twenty, and there was nothing he could do about any of it now.

"My mom likes Gordy as well. He kept her company after I was deployed. She said it eased her loneliness while I was gone." Gordy had to be pushing seven now, although Clancy didn't know his exact age. And he was glad he could spend the dog's remaining years with him. Staying away had been the easier choice, but he truly believed that coming home was now the right one.

Hollee turned away, wrapping her arms around her waist. "Are you ready to see Ava?"

Damn. Had his mention of his mom's loneliness reminded her of her own loss?

"You don't have to come if you don't want to."

She turned back. "I do. She's my friend, although I should have been checking on her more. It's time I made amends for that."

Maybe it was time he made amends too for the way he'd behaved. He might have been trying to do the right thing but had ended up hurting her, according to what Ava had said all those years ago. His sister had not been happy with him. But that was okay. He hadn't been happy with himself.

He moved closer and tipped her chin up. "About what I said all those years ago—"

"Don't. Please." Her whispered words shook.

"I just wanted to say I'm sorry."

Shimmering green eyes looked into his, and she opened her mouth as if to say something before shaking her head. "You have nothing to be sorry for. We were both kids."

Yes, they had been. He paused, then decided to ask a pivotal question. "Are we good?"

"Of course." Her chin went up, and she pulled away. "Shall we go?"

Once outside his sister's room, which was no longer in the maternity ward for the safety of the other new mothers, they donned surgical caps and gloves once again. Ava was sitting up in bed, a pillow pressed over her stomach, probably to ease the pain of the incision. She looked pale and drawn, but she smiled when she saw them. "Did you get to see her?"

"We did. She's beautiful."

"I didn't get to hold her. Or even get a good look at her."

Hollee smiled. "Well it's a good thing I snapped a couple of pictures then, isn't it?"

"You did?"

Ava said what he'd just thought. He hadn't noticed her taking pictures.

"Of course." She took her phone out of one of her pockets and punched a few buttons and then held it for Ava to see.

"Holy Moly! I did that?"

"You did indeed, honey." Hollee started to touch her, before thinking better of it.

Ava looked up at him. "Being an uncle suits you. You should see your face."

"What do you mean?"

"Come look."

He wasn't sure he wanted to, but to say no was bound to make both of them wonder why. So he went around to the other side of Holly and glanced at the images as she scrolled through them.

Hell. He looked like he was in love. Well, that's because he was. That tiny creature was his niece. It was normal to have a goofy grin on his face.

"Too bad you caught my bad side."

Their heads both came up at the same time. Ava spoke first. "Don't say that. You look fine, doesn't he, Hollee?"

He'd meant it as a joke, but evidently it fell flat. And he certainly didn't want Hollee to feel trapped into making some banal comment about his scar. Again. So he held up his hands to show capitulation. "Okay, I'm sorry. I won't say it again."

It did seem kind of incongruous that a plastic surgeon wouldn't have his own scars fixed or resurfaced. It would be easy enough to make them fade further into the background. But the reconstructions Clancy did were things that resulted from injuries or congenital conditions and he wanted his patients to love themselves, even if their after-surgery results weren't that of an airbrushed model. Not that he was the greatest example of loving himself either. Jacob had given him a pointed reminder of that a few days after he'd kissed Hollee.

I'm not like you, Mr. Bigshot. I'm a one-woman kind of guy, and between you and me, I'm crazy about Hollee, so don't go getting any ideas about adding her to your collection.

He'd never looked at himself that way, but evidently it was how Jacob—and maybe lots of other people—had seen him. It had been enough to make him pull back and put a stop to things with Hollee before he'd got in any deeper and ended up hurting her.

According to Ava, though, he'd ended up hurting her anyway. But, as he'd seen for himself, she'd recovered, and Jacob had gotten his wish.

Ava bent her head to the side, cracking her cervical joints. "They tell me that Jen-Jen is doing well."

Despite her illness, her personality refused to be squashed. She'd always been a firebrand, but Clancy had been fiercely protective of her when they had been kids, even though she would have clobbered him if she'd known.

"Jen-Jen? Is that really what you're going to call her?"

"How about Jenny J.? Or J.J.? No?" There was a happiness in her grin that he hadn't seen in a while, despite the evidence of exhaustion in her face. Now wasn't the time to approach her about her new daughter's middle name. But he would have to make a point to tell her. And soon.

"I personally like Jen-Jen."

"Hmm…" Her smile faded. "It's still so sad when I think of Jacob as being gone forever."

Hollee tucked her phone away, her head down, not looking at either of them.

"Yes, it is." He shifted and decided to change the subject. "Any idea when the baby can come home?"

"She needs to gain some weight obviously, but her lungs are strong. I heard her cry before they rushed her away." She shut her eyes and then looked at him. "I have to tell you it was the most beautiful sound I've heard in my life."

"I can imagine. When we saw her, she seemed…content." In fact, he'd been a little worried about how quiet she was, but Ava's words made him feel better.

"She really is beautiful." Hollee smiled, but this time it seemed a little forced.

It had to be hard hearing people talk about her late husband. Which was another reason he wanted to talk to Ava about the name, although he wasn't sure why it mattered. It mattered to him, though. Jacob had betrayed Hollee in the worst possible way. A one-woman man? It seemed that had been a lie. The last thing he wanted was for his niece to bear the man's name.

He took hold of one of his sister's toes through the blanket and gave it a wiggle. "We'd better let you get some rest, but I'll come see you tomorrow." He was careful not to include Hollee in that. She could set up her own visitation schedule.

"And since I worked the night shift, I'd probably better go home and try to get some rest," she said.

"Will you come back tomorrow too?"

"If you want me to."

Ava nodded. "Of course I do. And about what I said earlier, when I was in the delivery room…" Her glance shot to him before moving back to Hollee. "I was just scared and wasn't thinking straight."

"Whatever it was, it couldn't have been too important, because I can't even remember you saying anything."

"Good." She lay back against her pillows, eyes closed.

"Do you need anything?" Hollee asked. "Water? Something to eat?"

"I'm just incredibly sleepy right now."

"We'll get out of your hair, then." This time Hollee did touch her arm. Probably because she'd put her phone away and was about to shed her gloves. "Get some shut-eye now, because you'll soon be taking care of that precious little girl."

They left the room, and he couldn't help but ask, "What did she say that she was so upset about?"

"She wasn't quite coherent because of the fever. And since she doesn't want me to remember, it's probably just as well, don't you think?"

"I guess so. Well, I'll see you when I see you."

"Yep. I'm off to dreamland."

By herself. At least he assumed she would

be. The thought stopped him. Maybe that's why she seemed so uncomfortable whenever any reference to Jacob was made. She hadn't remarried or she'd have a ring on. Or maybe not, since jewelry could harbor germs, or hold them against the skin, in the case of a ring.

He watched her walk away, realizing he had more questions than when he'd started working at the hospital. And despite the fact that it shouldn't bother him, he was finding that it did. Very much. He wasn't sure how to unravel that. Or if he should even try. The only thing he could do was avoid her as much as he could—until they boarded their bus and drove off into the sunset together. Along with about twenty other people and a whole lot of medical gear.

Ugh! Hollee could not believe it. She and Clancy had joked about giving their dogs a play date and a week later she spotted him at the dog park at exactly the same time as her! Fortunately, he was some distance away and hadn't seen her yet. He was talking to some woman who was standing way too close, her Afghan hound looking tall and elegant, much like her owner, who was almost as tall as Clancy. And the way the woman looked at him, laughing at something he said...

A sick feeling rolled around the pit of Hollee's stomach as memories of the past flooded back. She guessed some things never changed. The nurses would probably also be fawning all over him soon enough.

Jacob had once joked that she'd dodged a bullet by being able to see through Clancy. Unfortunately, that hadn't been the case. But there'd been no way she would have admitted that to her husband.

Could she bear watching him make the rounds at the hospital in a way that had nothing to do with patients?

She should just turn back around and head toward her car, but when she tried to tug Tommie in that direction, her dog planted her feet, head whipping around as if to say, *What is this, human? A trick?*

"No trick, sweet girl. Just a big old dose of self-preservation."

Okay, if she couldn't retreat, she could simply head toward an obscure corner of the park and wait there until he left. Surely she could keep Tommie occupied until then.

She had a ball thrower and a tote bag that held an old soft quilt that her grandmother had made. She could just sit on the grass, ignoring Clancy and enjoying the day with no one being any the wiser. Except Clancy took out his phone and put it up to his ear, giving the woman with him an apologetic shrug, and the woman handed him something before heading on her way.

The sick feeling turned into something big and ugly. She would bet there was a phone number on that slip of paper.

Suddenly Gordy—wasn't that his name?—jerked to the right. Clancy, who wasn't expecting that or else was distracted by his call or the woman or both, careened sideways, landing right on his lean behind.

And it was lean. Just as lean as it had been ten years ago. Because, shamefully, she'd just looked.

Gordy broke free just as the woman and her fancy dog came back over and offered a hand to Clancy. Surprisingly, he didn't accept it, just hefted himself back up, but it was too late to catch Gordy, who was moving across the grass, his pudgy little legs moving like pistons. Behind him trailed his leash.

"Damn." The dog was headed in her direction!

About that time Clancy's gaze met hers and he cocked his head, bending over to retrieve his phone and the paper. He then started moving...fast, giving his new friend a quick wave as he left her behind. Within ten strides he'd caught up with his dog, snagging his leash and putting a stop to his flight, such as it was.

She realized, despite what she'd just witnessed, she was grinning like a loon. Because of Gordy, she told herself. Not because the incident had foiled the woman's attempt to hold Clancy's attention.

He made his way toward them, not saying anything as he let his dog sniff Tommie. Thankfully her dog was as friendly as his seemed to be. "Looks like they hit it off," he said. "I didn't realize you came to this park."

To his credit, he didn't look behind him to see what had happened to the woman he'd been talking to. It looked like she'd given up, since she was now walking in the opposite direction.

"I do." She was pretty sure that wasn't something to be celebrated. "Is this the park closest to you?"

Unfortunately that came out sounding like an accusation, when she hadn't really meant it to.

If he heard it, though, he didn't acknowledge it. Instead, one corner of his mouth tilted up. "Yes, actually it is. I've been here a couple of times."

That made her smile fade. Had he already met up with the same woman on other occasions?

She decided to hit neutral and change the direction of her thoughts. "How are Ava and the baby doing? Has she decided what to call her?"

Hollee was off today, and when she'd checked in on them yesterday, the pair had been doing well, with Ava finally being allowed to see her baby.

"Nope. So far J.J. and Jen-Jen are her favorites." Clancy suddenly frowned and looked closely at something. "Is your dog's eye okay? She's squinting."

Glancing down to check, she shook her

head. "She's actually missing that eye. Glaucoma," she added.

"I thought glaucoma was treatable. She had the eye removed?"

"It manifests differently in dogs. She'd had it for a while before her former owners had it checked. It was too late to save her vision and was causing considerable pain. She's adjusted quite well." She reached down to ruffle Tommie's fur. "We're hoping to retain the sight in her other eye as long as possible."

She hesitated, the tote on her shoulder starting to get heavy. "I brought a blanket—do you want to sit with us for a while?"

There was a noticeable pause on his part, then he lifted one shoulder, whether in irritation or a shrug, she wasn't sure. "We don't want to impose."

The words made her heart ache. Maybe he wanted to go back and find that woman.

Okay, she needed to answer this carefully. "I noticed you were talking to someone. I'll understand if you have other plans."

"Nope. No plans at all. Anyway, I think our dogs are enjoying each other's company."

A huge rush of relief washed through her, although it was ridiculous. He might not want to go find Ms. Afghan Hound right this minute, but he could always call her later. Or someone else would come along. She could pretty much depend on that.

That was okay, though, because Hollee wasn't interested in him like that. Not anymore, so there was no reason to sit here dwelling on it.

Why not just enjoy his company and not worry about the other stuff?

"I think so too. We can go over to one of the quieter areas, so they can stay out of everyone's way, if that's okay."

"Yes. Thanks. Gordy and I didn't think to bring anything to sit on."

More likely, he didn't feel the need to sit down, but since her legs had been feeling a little shaky ever since she'd spotted him, she'd better do something about it quickly.

That scar on his face drew her attention time and time again. He had to know she was staring at it. But it wasn't out of pity. She was fascinated by the changes that had taken place in him since the time she'd known him. Ten years had layered his face with a cynicism that hadn't been there before, the scars just adding to that feeling. It also added to that air of danger he'd carried with him back then. She'd used to fantasize about riding on that motorcycle of his, and she'd finally gotten her chance when he'd given her a lift home the night of the kiss. She'd been pressed tight to his back, her arms wrapped around his waist, and… *God…* He'd been lethal to her senses back then, and it seemed he still was. So much so that she'd done her best to avoid him in the days since little Jennifer's birth.

The man was gorgeous. And seeing him interacting with his sister's baby—the sheer devotion on his face—had opened a compartment in her brain that she'd thought was forever nailed shut. Why had he kissed her if he'd had no intention of asking her out on a date? Had he found her somehow inferior to the other girls he'd gone out with?

Her eyelids clamped closed for a second. That was a question to which there was no answer. And ultimately she'd chosen a different path. But one that hadn't necessarily turned out much better. But seeing him interact with that woman a few minutes ago had been a good wake-up call about why she needed to be careful.

She forced her attention to her surroundings. "How about over to our right? It's pretty empty."

"Looks good." He lifted the tote off her shoulder, fingers lightly brushing the side of her neck as he did so. A shiver erupted from that tiny contact, setting off her inner seismograph. It started frantically scribbling a warning that she'd better heed.

You need to sit down. Now.

She headed off in that direction, urging Tommie to follow. She did, but not without a shrill wail of protest. Hollee rolled her eyes.

"Not you too," she muttered. "One of us has to keep our heads, girl. This is a man who doesn't stick around for long. Don't count on his dog being any different."

A minute later they arrived at their destination, Clancy having to go more slowly in deference to Gordy's shorter strides. "Could you hold him for a minute?"

She took the dog's leash as he removed the quilt from the tote and tossed it open, allowing it to flutter toward the ground. Why did the man make everything look effortless? He took the ball and its thrower and set them on one corner. "That blanket looks handmade."

"The quilt? It is. My grandmother made it. She used it for picnics and so did my mom. Now it's mine." She didn't think it would last another generation, though, as it had been mended more than once. But she couldn't bring herself to leave it in a cabinet unused. It just seemed wrong. And since she was an only child, and there were no prospects on the horizon, it didn't look like there would be a next generation. A pang went through her.

"Nice."

He took Gordy's leash again and motioned for her to sit first. She did, smiling when Tommie immediately tried to plop in her lap. She'd never quite grasped the fact that she was a big dog. Bigger than laps were made to accommodate. But that hadn't stopped her yet.

Clancy toed off his tennis shoes and sat his jeans-clad form on the other side of the quilt. Gordy didn't try to crawl in his lap, she noted. He, evidently the better behaved of the two, sat beside his owner, his tail wagging back and forth.

Sucking down a chilly burst of air, but glad the weather had warmed up enough to allow this kind of outing in December, she allowed her muscles to finally relax now that her legs had stopped their quivering. "By January this will be impossible, so we'd better enjoy it while we can."

He set Gordy's leash on the quilt beside him. "Oh, I plan to enjoy every second I get."

Giving him a sharp look and finding his attention focused in the distance, she decided he wasn't talking about her but about the weather.

She started to remove Tommie's leash, since the park allowed it, then stopped. "If I let her go, will it bother him?"

"No. If she won't run off, I'll take his leash off too. He has a tendency to play follow the leader."

"Tommie pretty much sticks to me like glue."

Once freed, the dogs came to the center and sniffed each other again before moving into the nearby grass. Gordy rolled, while

Tommie sat and kept watch. It looked like she wasn't going to have to keep Tommie entertained after all. The animals looked perfectly content to romp nearby.

"How are you settling in at the hospital?"

He leaned back on his elbows. "It's a big change from what I'm used to, but I'm enjoying it. Obviously, I get more pediatric cases here than I did in the military."

"Those have to be hard."

He shifted to look at her. "They're different. A lot of them are due to accidents or burns, which definitely make you stop and think."

"Think? About what?"

"About what would have happened if things had turned out differently. About the long-term effects of a split-second decision."

Long-term effects? Oh, those were very real. One kiss had turned her world upside down and then dumped her onto her backside. It had been a heartbreaking lesson to learn: Don't let your impulsive side take control. Ever. Something she'd been very conscious of. It's one reason she hadn't dated since Jacob had died. She didn't want to take a chance on love, only to find out she'd made a mistake. Again.

Ugh. This was ridiculous. She hadn't thought of this stuff in years.

Maybe that wasn't exactly true, but it's what she needed to do: stop thinking about it. Those decisions were over and done with, and like Clancy had talked about with those injuries, they were irrevocable.

She fingered the stitching on the quilt. "I guess the same thing is true in labor and delivery. I've seen my share of surprise pregnancies. The parents' attitudes make the difference between it being a blessing or a burden. Like you said, split-second decisions carry consequences that follow you. For a long time."

Clancy stared at her, and it dawned on her that this time her tying something to the past hadn't just been in her head. She'd done it out loud, and he'd caught her. Only she hadn't done it on purpose. It just came out.

"Yes, they do."

Forcing herself to concentrate on the dogs, who were now lounging in the grass sunning themselves—Tommie's belly on full display, while Gordy's head was up, his eyes closed. "Well, they're sure enjoying themselves."

"They are."

She smiled. "So am I. I guess we got our play date after all." She quickly nodded toward the dogs. "Or theirs, I should say."

Despite her earlier thoughts, it really was nice just to sit beside him and soak in the sun. The only impulsive decision here had been to stay when she'd wanted to run. And it wasn't proving to be as disastrous as she'd feared.

"I appreciate you letting us crash your party."

She laughed. "I don't think Tommie is complaining too much."

"Neither is Gordy." He thought for a minute. "If you wanted, Tommie could stay at my place so your mom wouldn't have to move in with her. I'm sure my mom wouldn't mind feeding them both and letting them out."

"So you've decided to go?"

"It looks like Ava and the baby will be fine so yes."

She thought for a minute, trying to process what he'd just said and the fact that he'd suggested the dogs stay together. Her mom loved Tommie and she was pretty sure she'd be devastated to have to change her plans. "My mom's looking forward to spending time with Tommie. Maybe Gordy could come stay at my place."

He looked at her, frown in place. "Are you sure? He can be a little stubborn, as you saw earlier."

"Really? Well, my mom's put up with my stubbornness for twenty-seven years. I think she can handle Gordy."

"Gordy would probably like the company, actually. My mom still works, so she can't spend the whole day with him. But he can certainly survive. Ask your mom first, though, and see what she says."

"I will, but I already know it won't be a problem. So just plan on it. Besides, your mom will probably be busy with her new grandbaby. You can drop him off on your way to the hospital the day we leave."

"I can give you a ride, so we don't end up having to leave both of our vehicles at the hospital, if you want."

Okay, so she hadn't bargained on riding

over with him, but what was she going to say? No, I won't ride with you?

"Or I could give you a ride."

She only realized her chin was now sticking out defiantly when he tapped it. "You're right. Your mom can definitely handle Gordy."

"Very funny." But she did tuck her chin back in its normal position.

They spent the next half hour talking about things at the hospital and the trip, Clancy asking her if she'd ever practiced medicine in a disaster area.

"No, never. But as far as medicine goes, I imagine it'll be more about the big picture than the minutiae we worry about at the hospital, but that's not always a bad thing. Sometimes you just have to work with what you have, something we don't always learn in medical school."

"True. We don't always learn that in life either."

"No, we don't." Something Hollee would be smart to remember. If she could remember not to focus on the minutiae or try to "fix" things between her and Clancy, maybe they could learn how to relate to each other on a professional level and leave their personal feelings in the past.

Was that even possible? Especially with the season of mistletoe fast approaching? Would she need to perpetually be on the lookout for those traitorous sprigs? It was the time of hope. And kisses. Lord knew, she'd fantasized over that kiss long after it had happened. And now with him sitting beside her, his shoulder periodically brushing hers, it was hard not to go back and remember what it had been like to obsess over every little thing about him. The earthy scent that clung to his clothes. The smooth, warm leather of his jacket against her cheek as he'd given her a ride home on his bike. The heady anticipation of his lips as they'd ever so slowly descended…

God. She could feel that kiss all over again. A spike of panic went through her, going deep and lodging there.

Please, don't start wanting him again, Hollee.

How was she going to survive two weeks with him in Bender? Or seeing him for hours on end day in and day out?

She had no idea. But she'd better figure

out a coping strategy, and quickly. Or those long-term effects of a split-second decision that Clancy had talked about earlier could end up happening again. And if it did, she'd be in danger of it haunting her for the rest of her life.

CHAPTER FOUR

STRAINS OF CHRISTMAS music came down the corridors as Hollee headed toward the pediatric ward, telling her that Santa Claus was coming to town.

He actually *was* coming to town. Arlington Regional's part of town, anyway. It was always one of her favorite times at the hospital. They had a separate room set up with a huge Christmas tree and enough space to hold a hundred people. It was their way of giving back to the community. Patients current and past could come by for the next four Saturdays leading up to Christmas and get their picture taken with jolly Old St. Nick himself—played by whichever staff member happened to be available on any given weekend. Presents were piled high around the tree, courtesy of a grant given by a local business, one who'd been doing this for the last ten years.

Ten years. Her eyes closed. The year she'd gotten married.

Over and done with, Hollee. Stop dwelling on it.

She hadn't been. She'd actually been getting on with her life. Until Clancy had walked back into it. Only he hadn't known she was working at the hospital. She'd seen the shock on his face when he saw her in that corridor. He'd definitely not planned to ever lay eyes on her again.

And who could blame him? She'd never tried to contact him after Jacob died. Or speak to him after the funeral. She only had the small bits of information that Ava had mentioned over the years.

She turned the corner and those thoughts died, a smile taking over. The music was louder in here. And the room was full of children and laughter. Some of the kids wore wristbands signifying they were patients, and some didn't.

And there was Santa, sitting on what looked like a throne. A red velvet chair with ornate gold scrollwork that someone had dug up at a local thrift store and reupholstered. It had been in use for as long as most people could remember. But Santa Claus's identity changed each week.

There had to be pillows under that red suit, because this Santa didn't have anything that "shook like a bowlful of jelly." Despite the long white beard that covered the area under his nose, the man's face had no extra flesh. It was firm and carved, and there was a deep, deep furrow between his...

She peered closer, her mouth going suddenly dry.

It couldn't be. There was no way he would have agreed to be Santa.

Then again, the requests usually came from the hospital administrator, a hard man to turn down. Not because he was harsh and insisted, but because he had a quiet way of somehow convincing people to do what he wanted. Mainly because it was normally for the good of the hospital. Or morale. Or their patients. Even though this was a private hospital, Neil was really good at making this about health care rather than the almighty dollar. He'd even been known to go to bat against insurance companies when they refused to cover life-saving procedures. And since the board had kept him on, they must agree with the way he ran things.

But Clancy? As Santa?

The one thing she couldn't imagine him saying was "Ho, ho, ho!"

But there was a sexiness about him that came through, despite the oversized clothes. It was there in those dark eyes. In the slight way his mouth kicked up to the side when he smiled. Or maybe she was the only one who noticed those things. She doubted it, though. Women had always paid attention whenever he was around.

It wasn't just his body, though. It was the way he carried himself—the way he moved and talked. Even when he'd reclined on her quilt at the dog park, he'd been completely at ease with himself—a kind of self-confidence that bordered on arrogance, but stayed just this side of it. It was what had caught her attention and carried her beyond mere friendship when she, Jacob and Ava had been teenagers.

She hadn't cared about the consequences back then. Until Ava had pointed out that mistletoe and sent the events that followed spinning out of control. There'd been no coming back from that. Not as friends.

His eyes swept the room and caught her staring. That bushy white brow cocked at her in challenge and, sure enough, the left side of his mouth curved. Damn. The man would be sexy even when he was eighty.

She couldn't contain a small laugh and a shake of her head that she hoped conveyed her disbelief at seeing him in that chair. She pointed at him and mouthed, *You?*

One of his shoulders gave a half shrug. Then Neil got up on the stage, kicking up a bit of fake snow as he did so.

They'd done a great job on the decorations, and not just the snow. It was the whole atmosphere. There was a winter scene that boasted twinkle lights and huge shimmering Christmas ornaments. Some of those ornaments had been tossed haphazardly around the tree, as if they'd fallen and rolled into their spots. A tall snowman—a crazy patterned scarf knotted around his neck—stood off to the right, one bony stick arm raised in welcome. Someone had stuffed a set of lights inside him that changed color in time with the music. Which was now sounding off the names of Santa's reindeer.

It hadn't snowed in Arlington this year, but Hollee hoped, for the sake of the children, that whoever oversaw the weather sent a dusting of the white stuff their way before Christmas.

The administrator thanked everyone for coming. "We need a couple of staff members to be elves and pass out the presents. I see Hollee and Kristen out there. Would you two mind coming up?"

Oh, God. Why on earth had she stopped in here?

With the trip, she'd miss out on at least two of the Saturdays at the hospital, and who knew if her schedule after she got back would leave time to pop in? Besides, she'd been called on to be an elf before. It was no big deal. Or at least it shouldn't be.

But she'd not played elf to this particular Santa before. And wasn't sure she wanted to now.

Especially since Santa's lips were curved up in a smile that was full of mischief. And those lips were…

What? What exactly were they? A thread

of irritation ran through her. She kept circling back around to the same issue.

That stupid kiss should have only been a tiny blip on the radar.

But it was a blip that seemed to keep coming back to haunt her. And now she was one of his elves.

The only thing she could do was to play along. This was for these kids. Not for her.

She headed for the stage, meeting Kristen halfway. She forced a smile. "Can you believe we got sucked into this?"

The brunette, probably five years younger than she was, laughed. "And yet we keep coming back for more."

"Yes, we do."

Kristen bumped shoulders with her. "You have to admit it's fun to get to see the kids' faces up close and personal. And this week's Santa is pretty dreamy."

Her stomach plummeted. Of course Kristen had noticed. How could anyone in their right mind not see past the costume to the man himself? It was a good reminder of all the reasons Clancy was out of her league. He always had been. She'd just been too young to recognize it ten years ago.

Neil was talking about the logistics as they got onto the stage. She was glad she'd worn her Christmas ornaments scrubs in honor of today's festivities. Afterward there would be refreshments. She was off duty for the rest of the afternoon, which was why she could even be here today in the first place.

And she was glad. Glad that she'd get to watch Clancy's reaction as kids came up and told him what they wanted for Christmas and then received a gift in return. Photos would be taken that would later be mailed home to the families, so they'd have a keepsake of the day. It was great for the hospital's image, but she was relieved that that's not what drove the event.

Neil's daughter had been a patient here at the hospital many years ago. The Christmas event had been the bright spot of her stay. The administrator had vowed he'd keep the tradition alive so that no child felt left out. He'd wanted to show there was a little bit of magic to be had during this season, even in a hospital.

Soon the parade of children started, and while Kristen was on the far side, handing gifts to each child after they finished their chat with Santa, Hollee had been stationed at Santa's right, making sure that each person got their turn. She ushered the next child, a boy of about five, to Santa and lifted him onto Clancy's lap. "Ho, ho, ho, what is it you want from Santa?" The words were aimed at the child, but they sent a shiver over her. Because what she wanted from this particular Santa wasn't a toy. Or a present of any type.

Her Christmases after she'd married had been fun and happy at first, but by their fourth anniversary the luster had faded. And then, once Jacob had died, she'd spent almost every Christmas at her folks' house. Their enthusiasm for the season had rubbed off on her, and Hollee had found herself welcoming Santa back into her life once again.

And this particular Santa?

The young boy who was currently with Clancy rattled off about twenty toys he wanted, making the man in the suit smile. "That's quite a list you have memorized. You're lucky Santa has a good memory too. I'll see what I can do."

Hollee directed them both to look at the camera. "Smile."

Smile. Something she was doing more

and more of. Not because she had to but because she wanted to. She was getting into the spirit of the event, just like she always did. Despite her initial reservations about being up here with Clancy.

Two hours later, the last child had given Santa his wish list, and Hollee was getting ready to slip away when Neil interrupted. "Let's get a picture of Santa with his helpers for the newsletter."

What? She'd forgotten about that part of it.

She swallowed. Kristen was already on Clancy's left, and he motioned her up. Trudging back up the steps, she stood like a statue, giving the most fake smile she'd ever drummed up.

The photographer looked through his lens. "Person on the right, can you get in a little closer? And maybe look a little bit happier about being with Santa Claus?"

Happier. This had nothing to do with happiness. She managed to sidle over about an inch, only to have the photographer make another gesture, bigger this time. Suddenly a hand was on her hip, dragging her close to Santa's side. Eyes wide, she looked down at Clancy just as he glanced up at her, his grin dark and wicked, making her mouth go dry as she instinctively leaned into him. The world seemed to fade away.

It was then that a couple of blinding flashes reminded her that someone was taking photographs. She hurriedly turned her face back toward the photographer and forced herself to smile again. Except he was already gathering his equipment.

What? That was it? Her face had to have been the craziest of crazies. She looked at Kristen to see her laughing at something Clancy was saying, and her smile suddenly deserted her.

It was like being at the dog park all over again. Was there a woman on this earth who was immune to his charm?

Evidently not, judging by the way Hollee herself had stared at the man just moments earlier, her gaze dropping to his lips.

And then her mind shifted to the music that was currently playing, and she rolled her eyes. Seriously? Well, some kid's mom might have been caught kissing Santa, but she was not about to join that particular club. Especially not now.

So before she could somehow incriminate herself even further, she decided to hang up her Santa's helper costume and leave Clancy in Kristen's more than capable hands. She cringed at the image that thought evoked.

Because if he started actively flirting with her, Hollee was afraid she might scratch the other woman's eyes out. Despite the fact that it should mean nothing to her. And it looked like she had her answer after all.

This Santa had no place in her life. Not now. And probably not ever.

CHAPTER FIVE

WHAT THE HELL had possessed him to pull Hollee toward him like that the other day? The thought had rolled round and round his thoughts until he was dizzy.

He'd been trying to help the photographer, he reasoned.

Sure he had. What he'd really tried to do was get his hands on her, like he'd been itching to do all afternoon. Watching her help those kids, her warm smile as each one of them passed by, had worn away at him. Chipping away like a lumberjack preparing to fell a tree.

And sure enough, the second his fingers had cupped the curve of her hip, he could hear the distant shout of *Timber!* as he'd come crashing to the ground.

He wanted her. Wanted to toss her onto

the nearest bed and do what he hadn't gotten to do ten years ago. He wondered if maybe he should sleep with her to get it out of his system, but that was not going to happen. The last thing he needed was to make a messy history even messier. No one, except he and Hollee, knew what had happened that night, although he sometimes wondered if Ava had somehow guessed, since she was the one who'd pointed out the mistletoe.

He'd been hard-pressed to hide his emotions after telling her the kiss had been a mistake. But, at the time, he'd felt Jacob had been right. So he'd made the break as definite as possible.

He'd have to be just as adept now, although there was no need. Not anymore. She wasn't interested in him. The way she'd sped out of the room after that photo told him all he needed to know.

He glanced at his watch. He was a few minutes early to his first appointment but decided to see if his patient was in her room. If he immersed himself in work, he could wipe everything else from his mind.

The phone on his hip buzzed, and without

stopping what he was doing, he shifted it so he could see the screen. Hollee?

What the hell? It was almost as if she'd known he was thinking about her.

Pulling the phone free, he put it to his ear. "Hey, what's up?"

"I need you down here."

"What?" His brain stalled for a second, almost missing her next words.

"We have a problem in Maternity. Can you come?"

His thoughts sidestepped back to reality, although he couldn't imagine why they would need him. But she wouldn't have called if it wasn't urgent. "I'll be there in three."

Hanging up, he changed his route and headed for the elevator.

He reached the third floor and exited, glancing in both directions before seeing Hollee waving at him from the end of the hallway. She looked pretty upset. "What is it?"

"We have a situation. A newborn with a cleft palate. The mom came in with full-blown eclampsia and gave birth. She won't believe us when we say it can be fixed. If we can't get her blood pressure down, we're in danger of losing her."

Now that he listened, he did hear a disturbance down the hall. "Is her obstetrician here?"

"He's in there. But he thought if you came, you could explain the repair procedure to her and it might calm her down."

"And the baby?"

"She's in the nursery. Every time she caught sight of her, she just started up again. The husband is in there, but he's not much help. He almost passed out during the delivery."

"Okay. Can you bring the baby but stay just outside the door? Let me talk to her, and then we'll go from there."

She touched his arm. "Thank you. You'll understand when you see her."

Clancy knocked on the door she'd indicated and then pushed it open. Dr. Brouchet waved him over. "Marilyn, I've asked our plastic surgeon to talk to you about Sara, okay?"

The wailing he'd heard outside the door decreased in volume, becoming pained whimpers instead. The young woman was curled in on herself but shifted her eyes to look up at him. Her face was wet with tears.

"Hi, Marilyn, I'm Dr. de Oliveira. Congratulations on your new little one." No answer, but the crying had stopped, so she was listening. "I hear that she might need a little surgery. I haven't seen her yet, but I assure you I can help her."

"It's my fault." The soft voice was filled with a terrible conviction that tugged at his gut.

"Why do you say that?" He didn't want to jump to offer platitudes before he knew the situation.

"I… I…"

Her husband, who'd been standing silently beside her, touched her shoulder. "Tell him. It's okay." His voice was shaky—hesitant— like he knew something awful was coming.

"I—I was on drugs…heroin…when I got pregnant. Only I was too high to realize I wasn't having a period." She glanced at her husband. "We both were. And— Oh, *God*! It suddenly hit me, and I took a test. Afterward, we both went to rehab and got clean, but it was too…too late. My baby is *paying* for what I did. For what *we* did." Tears spilled over onto the pillow, but the hysteria wasn't there, like it had been.

Unfortunately, she was right. Addiction of any type during the first trimester could interfere with fetal development. But the fact that they'd both quit—had gotten help—showed how much they cared about this baby.

"She wasn't born addicted, because you both did the right thing. That's huge," he said. "And from what I've been told, she just has a cleft palate. Something very, very repairable."

Marilyn blinked up at him. "You promise?"

"I've asked the nurse to bring her, so I can look at her with you in the room. Is that okay? I'll give you my honest assessment."

Her hands started twisting together in a way that said she was about to get agitated again, so Clancy cut her off. "I can help her. Your baby isn't suffering, and I admire you, both of you…" He glanced up at the man. "…for getting help. You have to promise to keep up with whatever counseling sessions you've set up."

"We will." Her husband reached down and

took one of his wife's hands and squeezed it. He knelt by the bed and looked into her eyes. "Let him show us. She's our responsibility now. Our little girl. We need to do right by her."

Marilyn nodded then looked up again, a sudden frown appearing. "What happened to your face?" As if realizing what she'd said, she quickly apologized, but Clancy waved it away.

"I was injured by a piece of shrapnel in Afghanistan." He smiled. "And, no, that isn't my work. I promise she won't look like me when I'm done."

She laughed. "It doesn't look that bad."

"Hey, I have to look at this mug every day in the mirror. I know exactly what it looks like."

Glancing at the monitors behind her, he saw that her blood pressure was coming down. It was still above normal, but not in the danger zone like it'd been when he arrived.

"Can I ask the nurse to bring her in?"

Marilyn nodded, while her obstetrician came forward. "I'm going to check on another patient. You'll be in good hands with

Dr. de Oliveira. I'll be back in about a half hour to look in on you."

"Okay."

He gave her a smile and headed past Clancy. "Call me if you need me."

"We'll be fine," he said. "Can you tell Hollee to come in?"

Dr. Brouchet shot him a quick look before nodding.

Since Clancy had only been at the hospital for a few weeks, the OB/GYN was probably wondering how he already knew one of the nurses well enough to call her by her first name. But it was too late to try to cover the slip.

A minute later, Hollee came in with the baby swaddled in a blanket that was pulled up on the side of her face. Smart move. That way, the family's second introduction could be done a little more gently.

He was struck by the soft glow of her eyes as she cradled the baby, murmuring softly to her as if it was the most natural thing in the world. Her hair slid over the side of her face, and she tucked it behind her ear before her glance came up and caught him staring. She bit her lip, color flooding her cheeks.

He swallowed the lump in his throat. She would have made a great mother. Her babies would have been gorgeous and, oh, so…

Cut it out. You're not here for her. Or for yourself.

He dragged his gaze away and forced himself to do what he'd come here to do, moving closer and studying the baby's face. The cleft was unilateral. He met Hollee's eyes, keeping a tight rein on his thoughts this time. "Do you know if it includes the palate?"

"Yes, but it's not a large space."

"Good. Let's bring her over to the bed."

Marilyn's husband was again on his feet, a wariness in his demeanor that needed to be addressed. It was really important for him to show support and love for his child, or he would risk Marilyn blaming herself for that as well. He caught the man's attention. "Your baby is beautiful." He said it with meaning, hoping that the man would catch his drift. He evidently did, because he gave a slight nod.

"Okay, Marilyn. I'm going to tell you how I normally repair babies with clefts like… Sara, wasn't that her name?"

"Yes." The response came as a whisper that was barely discernible.

"I like it. It fits her, don't you think so, Hollee?"

"Yes. I do." Her smile was warm and genuine. "I've always loved that name."

Would she have named her own baby Sara?

And here he was back where he'd started: on shaky ground.

He got down to business, detailing how he would go about closing the cleft and repairing the lip. He used general terms so that the mom wouldn't be more frightened than she already was. "Do you think you can hold Sara so I can show you?"

Marilyn's throat moved, and she glanced at her husband and then at Hollee and the bundle she held. "I think so."

Clancy nodded. "Go ahead and help her hold her baby, but stay close in case she needs a little extra support."

Doing as he asked, she carefully placed the baby in her mother's arms, keeping the blanket pulled high on the side closest to Marilyn. Then, much to his surprise, the baby's mom eased the cover down, looking into her newborn's still face.

"She's just…sleeping, isn't she?"

The heartbreaking question threatened to breach the wall of detachment he'd built after years of working in combat areas. "Yes. She's sound asleep. See? Her lip doesn't hurt her, but it will need to be fixed so that it's easier for her to nurse and eat."

"You're sure you can?"

"This is an easy fix." Unlike his mixed feelings about working with Hollee. "We'll put her under anesthesia so she can't feel anything, and in an hour or two she'll be as good as new. She won't remember a thing. She might have a tiny scar here…" He pointed from the open area of Sara's lip to her nose. "…but it will be barely noticeable. Not like mine."

Hollee gave him a sharp look that he ignored.

"Can I nurse her?"

"Let me talk to her pediatrician and see what his thoughts are, but I don't think that will be a problem."

Her face showed immense relief. "Can you do surgery today?"

"No. Not today. We want to give her a little time to adjust to her world. You'll be able to take her home once you're released, and then we'll probably do surgery when she's six to eight weeks old."

"That long?"

"We want to make sure she's strong and healthy. It's not dangerous to leave it for a bit."

Sara's mom kissed her baby's forehead, as her blood pressure continued to drop.

"Do you have any questions?"

"No." Marilyn looked at Hollee. "I'm so sorry for grabbing your arm like I did. I was scared."

"Don't worry about it. Giving birth is scary under normal circumstances and everything happened so quickly that you didn't have a lot of time to process what was going on."

Clancy frowned. Had she been hurt? She hadn't mentioned there being an altercation, just that Marilyn was upset. Her concern had been wholly for her patient and the baby. Not for herself.

He'd known Hollee when she was just beginning to know who she was. Now he was seeing her standing here as a competent, self-confident nurse who was good at what she did. If Jacob hadn't reinforced what Clancy had already believed about himself, would she be where she was now? Would she have fallen in love with him instead?

It was a question no one could answer. Maybe they would even be divorced by now. He doubted he was the easiest person to live with. He didn't show his emotions easily. Even now. *Especially* now, after everything he'd seen in the world.

He pushed all those thoughts aside. "Do either of you have any more questions?" He probably needed to get back to his first patient, as he was now running a few minutes late. But this had been important.

"I want you to do the surgery."

He smiled. "I wasn't planning on letting anyone else do it, so that's a good thing."

There was something about this young family that touched him. Sara's parents had a lot of growing to do, but he saw a lot of hope in the situation.

Marilyn reached over and gripped her husband's hand, tugging him closer. And, thank God, there wasn't an ounce of revulsion or fear in the man's face.

"Hollee, can you let me know when Sara is getting ready to be discharged? I have a little something for her from Santa's visit." If anyone deserved a fresh start, it was this couple.

"I will." The smile she sent him contained gratitude, relief and a touch of something else. Attraction?

Maybe he wasn't crazy after all.

As she walked him toward the door, Hollee peered up at him. "When did you want to meet with Mom about Gordy?"

"I guess it needs to be soon, since we're less than a week out."

"Okay, I'll let you know."

"That would be great." He nodded at the couple and said goodbye to them, and to Hollee, who mouthed, *Thank you, Clance*.

"Anytime," he said aloud. And for the first time since they'd met again he actually meant it.

CHAPTER SIX

HOLLEE'S MOM HAD just left. Thankfully the meeting had been more comfortable than he'd thought it would be. Just polite chitchat that had centered around the dogs, who were now tussling on the floor.

Clancy should leave too. But he'd had a long day, and it felt good to just sit and do nothing. And since nowadays that "nothing" tended to happen when he was alone, it felt good to have company.

"Hey, do you want to stay for dinner? Tommie and Gordy seem to be getting along really well, and this will give us a chance to see if there's any squabbling when we feed them."

He thought for a minute. Was that a smart idea? Maybe not. But if she was okay with sharing a meal with him, then what would it hurt?

"Actually, that sounds good. But I don't want to put you to any trouble."

"Trouble? Nope. Cooking's my mom's specialty, not mine. I was thinking of ordering takeout, if you're up for that. Chinese?"

This idea was sounding better and better.

"My favorite. On paper plates so there are no dishes?"

"A man after my own heart."

Except he wasn't. And taking the sentence apart and reading it literally, he wasn't after her heart. At least he shouldn't be. Not anymore.

But what was keeping them from going back to a time when they had been friends?

She went into the kitchen and came back with a takeout menu. "Would you mind ordering? I like just about everything from there, so you choose. I'm going to run and change my clothes."

At least she hadn't said she was going to slip into something more comfortable, because he was already feeling way too comfortable. He'd never really done "domestic" stuff with a woman. It was more like go out to eat and then go back to his apartment and then leave for work the next day. His companion for the night was always gone when he got back. It was how he liked it. Uncomplicated.

And for the last year or two it had been less than that, because he hadn't dated at all, and he wasn't sure why. He just didn't have the emotional energy anymore.

He perused the menu, scolding Gordy once when he took something away from Tommie. "You have to learn to share, buddy."

Really? Because not everything could be shared. Toys, yes. People, no.

Choosing something that sounded good, he was on the phone placing their order when Hollee came back in a pair of gray yoga pants and a dark T-shirt. He swallowed, forgetting what he was saying for a minute.

She'd slipped into something a little more comfortable after all.

Who in their right mind had ever criticized a woman for wearing those? The stretch in that fabric was just enough so it flowed over her hips and cupped that firm behind in a way that made his mouth water.

Friends, remember?

He did remember. But a little piece of him was waving a flag in protest.

He jerked his mind back to the person on the other end of the line, who was asking if there was anything else he wanted.

Ha! He wasn't touching that. But he'd already let his pause go too long without adding something.

"Could you throw a couple of fortune cookies in with that order? Thanks."

He paid with his credit card and noticed Hollee was signaling him from across the room. "Could you hold on for a minute please?" He glanced at her. "Is there something else you want?"

"No, but I invited you. I was going to pay for it when they got here."

"It's the least I can do for borrowing your mom for the next two weeks."

"Borrowing...? Oh, the dogs."

He finished up the order and then hung up. "They should be here in about twenty-five minutes."

"Perfect. I could use some wine. How about you?"

"That sounds good. I'll come help."

He followed her into the kitchen, doing his best not to watch the jiggle of her behind as she went, but, damn, it was hard. His friendship card was quickly getting lost in the shuffle.

The last ten or so years had been exceedingly good to her. She looked better now than she had back when he'd first noticed she was all grown up, something he could not say for himself. He knew the repeated trips into war zones had hardened him in all the wrong ways. Not to mention his scarred face.

Somewhere along the way he'd forgotten what life was all about. Maybe Jacob's death had reminded him that nothing in life was certain. Or maybe it was meeting Hollee again after all these years.

Meeting that young family with the new baby had given him a jolt. That couple had journeyed through a war zone of a completely different kind, but one that was just as devastating as any he'd seen during combat. Drugs senselessly claimed lives just as guns and artillery did.

Marilyn and her husband had given him a glimmer of hope, as strange as that sounded.

If they could come through what they had and learn to enjoy life again, then maybe he could too.

Maybe he could even find someone in the future and settle down and have a family.

When his eyes strayed to Hollee, he gave his head an inner shake. The time for that had come and gone, when he'd decided he wasn't the kind of person she needed. Although knowing what he did about his former friend, he wondered again if that had been the right decision.

Hollee opened a cupboard and stretched up high, grabbing a pair of glasses, her T-shirt pulling taut over one of her breasts as she did. And his mind was right back in the fray, giving the finger to his rationalizations.

Staying for dinner might just be a mistake after all.

She got a bottle of wine out of the fridge and handed him a corkscrew. "Why don't we feed the dogs before we eat dinner? Otherwise Tommie will make a nuisance of herself."

"So will Gordy."

By the time she'd put food down for each of them, he had the wine ready to go. And, surprisingly, the dogs were pretty compatible as far as eating habits went. They were both done in record time, leaving nothing for the other to devour.

"If you'll carry the glasses into the living room, I'll let them out for a while. Tommie's not a lover of winter, so she won't want to stay out long."

She called the dogs and opened the sliding glass door. Out they went.

"You don't have a tree up."

From what he remembered about Hollee's family, they were all about Christmas. He could remember his family being invited to their house for an annual holiday party. It had always been warm and welcoming... and decorated to the hilt. Hollee, however, had nothing up at all. Not a single strand of lights. It didn't seem in keeping with what he remembered of her.

"No. We'll be leaving for Bender pretty soon, and I've spent Christmas with my folks ever since... Well, for quite a while. I've been thinking, though, maybe I should start decorating again. Maybe next year."

Before he could respond, she disappeared into the back of the house before coming back carrying a huge pillow. "For Gordy. That's the one thing Tommie doesn't really like sharing. Her bed."

And Hollee? Did she like sharing hers?

Dammit, Clancy. Just stop it.

She dropped the new pillow beside the one that was already next to the fireplace. "Do you want me to turn it on?"

Blinking, he tried to decipher—

"The fireplace."

Of course. He should have guessed. But with his mind drifting down paths it shouldn't, everything was coming back with some kind of double meaning. "I'll leave that up to you."

"On, then." She took a remote and pressed something and flames leaped to life behind the glass. "Tommie loves lounging next to it."

"Since I don't have a fireplace, Gordy will have no idea what it is."

"So what about you? Did you decorate this year?"

He hadn't given it much thought. His places of residence had been so transitory that he hadn't invested in a tree or ornaments. "No. I didn't either, actually. Maybe

I will if I ever move out of the apartment into a house."

If. So he wasn't thinking of making his stay more permanent? Was he waiting to see how he handled civilian life before making a commitment to it? Well, that ship had pretty much sailed. He'd already gotten his honorable discharge. Getting back in would be an undertaking.

She sat on the sofa, and he handed her one of the glasses, then took his spot back on a nearby chair. Although her sofa was pretty long, he wasn't sure he was up to the challenge of being that close to her. The casual Hollee was sexier than the business Hollee, as evidenced by his reaction to her at the dog park. And his reaction right now.

Taking a sip, he sighed. "Thanks for asking me to stay. I was too tired to even think about dinner."

"Hard day?"

"You could say that. I had several emergency surgeries in a row, which is unusual."

"And I dragged you here for a meeting with Mom."

He grinned. "You didn't 'drag' me. It was

a good distraction. And I needed some down time."

"I'm glad you're staying then."

Was she?

Before he could unravel how he felt about that, a scratching sound at the patio door made him look up. Sure enough, it was Gordy.

Saved by the dog.

When she started to get up, he motioned her to stay where she was. "I'll get them."

He let the dogs in, and Tommie took one look at the fireplace and plopped down. Gordy followed, hesitating as if unsure what to do, so he called the dog over to the second pillow. For once, he did as he was asked.

Then the doorbell rang. "And that'll be our dinner," she said.

Once they had everything on the kitchen counter and had dished out the food, they made their way into the dining room. When Hollee held up the bottle of wine with her brows raised, he shook his head, although he was tempted to join her for another glass. "I'm driving home. Better not. I'll just have some water."

Over dinner they discussed various cases

and he caught her up on how Ava and the baby were doing, starting to relax as the conversation remained on neutral topics.

Then she took a sip of her wine, and her lips lingered on the rim of the glass for a second longer than normal. And just like that, neutral shifted back into drive.

"Well, I'm glad it turned out the way it did." She swirled the contents of her glass, and he held his breath. But all she did was stand and pick up her plate. "Done?"

"Yes, I'll help you clean up."

They had just dumped their paper plates in the trash, and she was getting ready to toss away the bag the meal had come in, when she glanced inside it. "We almost forgot!"

She held up one of the fortune cookies, hopping up on the counter top and handing him the other one.

He took it, even though he had a hard time thinking about anything other than how Hollee at that height was absolutely perfect. For a lot of things. She took another slow drink of her wine and then set the glass beside her hip.

Hell, he should leave.

She tore into the cookie's packaging, glancing at him as she did. "Aren't you going to open yours?"

"Yes." He leaned a hip against the counter and took his cookie from the wrapper, breaking it in half. Retrieving the tiny slip of paper, he popped part of the cookie into his mouth as he read his fortune.

His eyes widened, and something went down the wrong way. He coughed, trying his damnedest to disguise it as clearing his throat.

"Are you okay?"

"I just tried to inhale when I should have swallowed."

She laughed. "Not a good plan."

Here's hoping he could distract her. And himself. "So what does yours say?"

"Same old stuff. Your path to success will soon be revealed."

"I think you're already on the path to success." Maybe if he talked enough, she'd forget about his. "You're doing a great job at the hospital." He shoved his fortune into his pocket.

"Wait, what did yours say?"

So much for making her forget about it. "Same old stuff, just like yours."

"Read it, then. It's the best part of the meal."

It might have been, had they been young and optimistic and on their first date. But they weren't. And a lot of water had passed under the bridge since those days.

With a great deal of reluctance he reached into his pocket and pulled out the paper, even though every word was now burned in his skull. He pretended to look at it and debated whether or not he should just make something up. Except then she might ask to look at it, and right now his head was drawing a blank on other viable options.

"The past belongs to the past, time to make a new beginning."

She blinked, then licked her lips. "I guess you're already doing that."

"I am?"

"You just got out of the military. And now you're working at the hospital. Or were you thinking of something different?"

He was. Which was why he'd almost choked on that cookie. "Those fortunes are always a crapshoot. They could mean a thousand things."

Her bare feet which had been swinging back and forth were now planted on the flat surface of a drawer, one heel on the metal handle. Oh, Lord, he was in trouble. In very big trouble.

"Like what?"

"Oh, I don't know. Like the trip to Bender or any number of new beginnings."

She used a foot to nudge his leg, letting it rest there for a second. "Speaking of Bender, have you heard anything about our sleeping arrangements?"

The room suddenly got warm. "As in…?"

"Where we'll sleep, silly. I don't think there will be many hotels open for business. Will we be in tents, or what?" Her foot bumped his leg again.

Was she flirting with him?

"I don't know. I haven't heard anything."

"Hmm… I haven't either. What if there are communal showers? Are you taking swim trunks?" She gave a grin that was full of devilish intent, her foot landing back on the drawer front. "Talk about new beginnings. And new fodder for the hospital's rumor mill."

"I'm pretty sure they'll have separate showers." His voice came out half-strangled. He could think of all kinds of new beginnings that might stem from that kind of scenario. And the last thing he needed to picture was Hollee lathering herself in a hot steamy shower, bikini or not.

"I'm sure they— What's wrong?"

"Nothing."

And then she looked at him. *Really* looked at him. "Oh."

That one word changed the atmosphere in the room in an instant, her eyes going from the cool green of today's Hollee to something he recognized from ten years ago.

They stared at each other, and he swallowed, finding the act more difficult than it should be. A lot more difficult.

The fortune that was still curled in his palm seemed to burn his skin, making him remember exactly what he'd thought those words had meant. That what was in the past—*their* past—didn't matter. But it did.

Despite that, something inside him declared war on the rational part of his brain.

Her foot touched his leg, but this time it didn't bump and leave. It stayed. Slid a few inches and then stopped as if waiting for his response.

All of a sudden he wanted one thing. Hollee. On that counter. Naked.

He turned and bracketed her in, planting a hand on either side of her.

"What are you doing, Hollee?"

The look she gave him sent a spear right through him. How many times had he regretted his decision to stop at a kiss ten years ago?

Maybe she'd read his mind, because she replied, "We're two consenting adults. It doesn't have to be anything more, does it? I don't want it to be anything more."

And that settled it. Because neither did he.

His hands slid up her arms, and as if anticipating what he wanted, her legs parted, allowing him to come close. And hell if he hadn't been exactly right about the height of that counter top.

Cupping the back of her head, he slowly reeled her in, needing to draw this first contact out and make it last.

Her lips touched his, warm and moist

and just as sweet as he remembered. Only as soon as they came together, it was as if an explosion went off between them. Her arms wrapped around his neck and held him tight against her as their mouths suddenly clashed, tongues and teeth battling to take control of the situation.

And, sure enough, the feet that had been pressed to the vertical surface of the cabinets were now flattened against the backs of his thighs. Taking that as his cue, he gripped her hips and yanked her forward until there was full contact between them.

Her low, throaty moan sent a shudder through him, and his eyes closed, wanting to hold onto that sound and remember it forever. He hadn't heard anything that needy, that sexy in a long, long time.

Her hands moved to the back of his shirt and tugged it out of his waistband, the sensation of it being balled up in her fists making him hungry for her. He couldn't believe this was happening, didn't want it to stop.

Leaning back so that she could drag the shirt over his head, he found he already missed her mouth. As soon as she'd tossed it to the other counter, he took up where he had left off. Only she was now fumbling with his belt.

This wasn't the shy girl he remembered from the past. Then again, he wasn't the same cocky boy she'd once known. They were both adults now.

And as the adult he was, he was not going to stand there while she stripped him naked. Not without putting them on an equal footing.

He reluctantly broke the kiss and took hold of the T-shirt he'd admired a little while earlier and pushed it slowly up her torso and over her breasts. And confirmed that, yes, she did have a bra on, something very thin and lacy and delicious looking.

Soon the shirt was off, and his palms cupped her, the soft flesh filling his hands to perfection.

She reached behind her and unsnapped the bra, throwing it in the same direction as his shirt, before pressing herself back into his hands. His body ached, needing to touch her everywhere, even as his thumbs strummed over her. And when he covered one of those nipples with his mouth, she squirmed against him, her hands going to the back of his head and holding him in place.

There was so much he wanted to do, but it didn't look like she was going to give him that chance. There was a quickness to her breathing that seemed to border on desperation. So he let himself be swept along on the same wave she was riding, pulling back just long enough to grip the elastic of her yoga pants and slide them down, her hips lifting to help him. When her panties started to come with them, he decided to hell with it and helped them along.

He let both garments fall to the floor and then moved in close again, the thought of so little separating him from the place he wanted to be driving him to reach into his pocket and take out his wallet, securing protection.

"I want you naked," she whispered.

He was right about the change in her. This was a woman who wasn't afraid to ask. And he gloried in it. No games. No tricks. Just a man and a woman doing what came naturally.

A little tug inside his skull whispered a

word of caution, but he wasn't going to listen to it.

Instead, he kicked off his shoes and removed the rest of his clothes. And then he was there. Against her...having to hold himself back from taking her, condom or no condom.

But he wouldn't.

She handed him the packet, and he sheathed himself as her lips trailed tiny paths over his jaw, his chin, his throat, leaving molten lava in her wake. She whispered against the corner of his mouth. "Do it, Clance. Please."

There was no doubt about what she wanted. It wasn't more heated kisses, or a little more foreplay. She wanted the main event. And at her words so did he.

Aligning himself with the moist heat, he pushed into her in a rush, burying himself inside her. Her eyes fluttered closed, her fingers digging into his hair and pulling him to her.

Mouth? Or nipple? He wanted both. Kissing her deeply, he let his tongue play out the events that would soon unfold, working the kiss to a climax that he had to force his body not to follow. When he finished she was panting, trying to move her hips against him. Then he took the nipple he'd lusted after and started to move, tongue scrubbing over the tight bud, teeth holding her in place.

She whimpered, fingers gripping his hair, the sharp pull on his scalp just adding to his pleasure. He kept moving, setting a steady pace, even as everything in him was forging ahead, trying to find its own conclusion. Then her legs wrapped around his waist, using the leverage to up the ante, and changed the tempo and intensity to a crescendo.

Hollee was no longer asking. She was telling. She wanted more, and if he didn't give it, she was going to take it.

Well, honey, your wish is my...

He met her thrust for thrust, never stopping his contact with her breast. Every pump of his hips was hitting the right spot, if her moans and sinuous movements were anything to go by. His intent to reach between them and make sure she was getting as much pleasure as possible was stopped by the way her hands abandoned his hair and gripped his upper arms as if needing to anchor herself to him. It was a heady sensation and one he would never forget. Didn't want to forget.

He released her breast and glanced up at her. The sight of her head leaning against the upper cabinet, sliding upward with each thrust of his hips was the most decadent thing he'd ever witnessed. For a second he couldn't move his gaze. And then her eyes opened and caught him staring, her lips parting.

"Clance…"

Her breathing of his name was his undoing and suddenly he was thrusting into her at atomic speed, her cry warring with his groan as she contracted hard around his flesh. Over the edge he went, into the oblivion beyond, eyes jammed shut once again as pleasure poured over him, hot and wet and unbelievably long.

And then it was over, his movements slowing as things around him began to fall back into place. Her hands were again on the back of his head, but not frantic the way they had been, body softening as it accompanied his to the other side.

"That was…" Her eyes closed, and another tiny spasm gripped his flesh. "That was luscious."

Luscious. The word struck him, and he couldn't stop the chuckle that came out.

She frowned. "Is something funny?"

"Not funny. No. Not…not at all."

Her frown was still there. "Then what?"

"Luscious is not a word I've heard used before in reference to that."

She blinked. "And you've heard a lot of those words?"

He wasn't sure what to make of that. She didn't sound angry, but there was something there that had a little sting to it. Had she thought he'd been celibate all these years? "My share. As I'm sure you did as well."

With Jacob? Why the hell had he even said that?

He separated himself from her, unsure why they were even talking about this.

"I haven't been with anyone since my husband passed away."

And that did it. Hearing her call Jacob her husband made him turn and gather his clothes together. He knew exactly who she'd been married to. He didn't need anyone—especially her—to announce it to him. Especially after everything that had happened. After what Jacob had done.

If her aim had been to keep this simple and a one-time event, she'd just gotten her wish.

Only as he headed into the other room to get dressed, he wasn't sure exactly how he could use the word *simple* to describe what had happened between them. Because nothing in his life, including Hollee, had ever been more complicated than it was right now.

CHAPTER SEVEN

THE LAST TWO days had gone by with alarming speed.

Hollee was at the hospital with her bags, joining the others who were waiting on the bus that would take them to Bender. Rather than the tents she'd joked about staying in, FEMA had sent in small trailers to house emergency workers.

She hadn't actually talked to Clancy since that episode in her kitchen. By the time she'd dragged her clothes on and gathered her thoughts, plastering an empty smile on her face, he had gone, along with Gordy. Poor Tommie had stood at the door, whining after them.

"I know, girl," she'd said. "I think I just made a huge mess out of that.

Her emotions had already been starting

to fray and to hear him talk about what he had and hadn't heard during sex had made her snap. All of a sudden she'd pictured that woman at the dog park and the dozens of women he'd probably been with, and it reminded her of how casually he'd turned his back on her ten years ago. How he'd found someone else almost immediately afterward.

His behavior had devastated her, and she wasn't sure why. Had he changed in the intervening years? She had no idea, because she'd blurted out the first thing that had popped into her head. It had been a mistake.

So was what had happened between her and Clancy? When he'd asked what she was doing, she should have made something up. Instead, she'd practically begged him to stay, saying they were both adults. It might have been true, but they weren't two objective bystanders brushing shoulders as they passed each other on the sidewalk. They had a past. Not much of one, granted, but still.

They'd shared an intense, heady kiss one day, and the next thing she knew he'd dropped her like a rock. That should have warned her that having sex with him—

ever—was off limits. It was bound to make an awkward situation even worse.

And now she was going to spend two weeks with the man.

Thankfully she spotted Kristen getting out of a car with her bags and headed toward her, giving her friend a quick hug. "I'm so glad you got to come."

Kristen smiled back. "Me too!" Her friend flipped open a hospital newsletter. "And it looks like the hospital thinks you and the new doctor are getting along. *Really* getting along." She handed Hollee the paper, and she felt the blood rush from her head, her vision going white for a split second.

She and Clancy were on the cover. Well, not just them, there were a lot of other pictures as well. But the one of Clancy, her and Kristen was all she could see at the moment. And it was as damning as she'd thought it'd be. She and the plastic surgeon were gazing into each other's eyes, her mouth a round "O" of surprise, while Kristen smiled at them both. God. Just a couple of days ago, she'd joked about the communal showers and the rumors that could be set into motion.

It turned out it wasn't a shower that would set those wheels turning. It was a picture.

And the rumors would all be true.

Well, not exactly, because she had no intention of ever having sex with him again. She'd learned her lesson. At least she hoped she had.

"You were there. You know pictures don't always tell the whole truth."

"All I know is that I would have given anything to have one of those steamy glances aimed at me."

"You're crazy. There was nothing steamy about it."

Speaking of steamy, she sensed Clancy coming onto the scene even as she talked to her friend. Forcing her voice to sound more animated than she felt, she quickly changed the subject, aware that Kristen was still holding that newsletter. And it was still showing the damning cover. There was no way she could ask her to put it away without the other nurse reading more into it than there was, or without Clancy noticing and wondering why she was reacting so oddly. Maybe he'd already seen it and thought it was no big deal.

Kind of like their night together?

That thought hit her in the solar plexus and knocked the wind out of her for a second, because to her it *had* been a big deal. A very big deal. And that's what hurt the most.

She'd done all this talking as if their time together had been about two people having casual sex and then moving past it. Her problem was that she had trouble being objective when it came to Clancy de Oliveira. If she thought the sex would serve to close the book on that little crush she used to have on him, she was wrong. The book had crashed wide open instead, ripping a hole straight to the past. Then she'd had the gall to judge him for sleeping with other women. He had the right to live life the way he saw fit. How dared she act like he didn't?

Just as she'd run out of things to say to Kristen and had gotten the rundown on what their responsibilities were going to be, there was a call to load up the bus. Thank God. She didn't have to worry about facing him. In fact, she'd chosen the coward's way out and had left her mom to welcome Clancy and Gordy to her house. Hopefully that had gone well. She got on, sliding into the first empty seat she could find. Kristen sat next to her.

Clancy gave her a nod as he went by before he too sat down. In the seat directly behind hers. Great. Maybe she should have tried to find a time to meet with him and have it out, rather than just run every time she saw him.

Why did she need to, though?

They weren't involved as a couple, so she really didn't owe him anything. And he hadn't tried to contact her in the last two days either. So maybe that was how things were going to work. They'd just each stay in their own little corners of the world and not talk or have anything more to do with each other, except where Ava was concerned.

That made her incredibly sad.

No, sometime in the next two weeks she was going to make time to have a conversation with the man and see if they could get to a place where they were both okay, both on the same page.

About everything.

And at least she finally knew what it was like to have sex with him.

It had been fantastic. More wonderful than she ever could have imagined.

Ugh. And that just made it so much worse.

But she would find a way to make it better. Somehow. She just had to do it in the next two weeks.

After a six-hour bus ride, Clancy looked out at a scene of devastation. There were still huge puddles where the rivers had overflowed their banks and the smell of rot seeped through the closed windows of their vehicle, despite the cold temperatures.

Somewhere around ten trailers were lined up side by side, looking pristinely white compared to the neighboring mud-covered structures, many of them damaged by the tornado. Not a single sign of Christmas was in evidence.

Next to the trailers stood a huge wooden barn, which he assumed was being used for a staging area.

The bus stopped, and Hollee and her friend were two of the first people off. The other woman had left the hospital newsletter on their seat. He picked it up, so he could return it to her and caught sight of a picture of him and Hollee. He tensed.

It was a reminder of that day in the hospital—the place where he'd made his first big mistake. Right there in that room of Christmas cheer. Instead of letting the photographer handle the picture, he'd taken matters into his own hands in a very literal sense.

The memory had primed the pump and tickled the back of his skull every time he saw her, until it had finally gotten its way in her kitchen. The aftermath of that encounter hadn't been pretty.

He stepped off the bus and saw a small group of people shaking hands with the medical team. The weather was noticeably warmer than it had been in Arlington, but then they were further south. A little boy ran over to him, and turned his head, peering at the newsletter. "What's that?"

"Randy, leave the man alone." A grizzled figure came over and shook Clancy's hand. "Sorry about that. My son is excited that you're here, as you can tell."

"He's fine." He crouched in front of the boy. "Hi, Randy, I'm Clancy. This isn't anything that would interest you, but we have a few things that might. We'll tell you about them a little later."

The boy's father smiled. "We appreciate the help."

Clancy stood. "You live here in Bender?"

"I do. Rather, I did. Our house is gone. We're living with my sister and her family until we can decide what to do."

The man had a ring on his finger. "Your wife?"

"I lost her..." His throat moved and his voice stopped for a second. "I lost her and my daughter in the tornado."

"I'm sorry." Clancy had seen the physical evidence of the horror these people must have gone through, but hearing it spoken was a punch to the gut. He glanced at Randy, who probably didn't understand the full extent of what had happened, and a lump formed in his throat.

"Thank you. There are a lot of others in the same position. Whole families have been lost."

"I know nothing can bring your wife and daughter back, but we want to help however we can."

Someone motioned them toward the barn,

and he grabbed his bag, smiling at Randy and his dad as he headed in that direction.

Once inside the building, he saw that a small room had been fashioned, using partitions. Someone he didn't recognize climbed up on a platform. "Hi, everyone, and thanks for coming. I'm Matt Gormley, and I'm overseeing the medical portion of the disaster relief efforts for FEMA. We've got room assignments for you in the trailers you saw as you pulled in. There will be four people per two-bedroom trailer, but meals will be cooked and served in another area of the barn by volunteers."

He glanced around at them. "I'm not going to lie to you. We have a lot of hard work ahead of us, since the only hospital within fifty miles was wiped out by the series of tornadoes that came through. We're flying urgent cases to Mount Retour, but there are a lot of skin infections, damaged limbs and sickness that flowed in with the flood waters. We've had long lines ever since we started operations. We want to get all of you signed in and set up with badges today. Current volunteers go home tomorrow, and you'll be briefed by them in the morning."

He went on to let them know where they could find their posted hours of service and lodgings. Evidently part of the barn had more walls erected as a makeshift surgical room and several exam rooms, but they were warned that waiting times were very long and they were still triaging patients as they came in.

Clancy could relate to that, since it was what he was used to. Then they were dismissed and asked to go to registration and sign in

When he went outside, there was no sign of Randy or his dad, but he did see Hollee standing a few yards away.

What did she think of all of this?

He made his way over to her, her face revealing no sign of how the briefing had made her feel. But when he got to her, she gave him a stiff smile. "Did Gordy give you any trouble this morning?"

"No, if anything, he and Tommie seemed happy to see each other again."

"They hit it off." She bit her lip and glanced around before continuing. "Listen,

Clance, I'm really sorry about…everything that happened. I think we were both tired, and the wine…"

He'd only had one glass of the stuff, so he'd been stone-cold sober. And if she tried to pass this off as a simple reaction to alcohol, he wasn't going to be happy. But she was right about them both being tired. He remembered saying he was too tired to worry about dinner. In fact, the whole cascade of events leading up to what had happened was a kind of a blur in his mind. Unlike the actual time spent in that kitchen. That had scorched a path through his skull that would be difficult to erase.

"Like you said, it was a one-time thing. We both made it to the other side, so why don't we put it behind us?"

She gave a sigh, like a weight had been lifted off her shoulders. And maybe it had been. Heaven knew, he was happy to finally get this out in the open, since the way they'd left things had been eating away at him.

"I would love that." She turned toward him and held out her hand. "Friends. Again?"

They would probably never make it back to the friendship they'd had as kids. But maybe they could somehow forge something new based on mutual respect and admiration. His fortune cookie's message came back to him: the past belongs to the past. Maybe this time he could leave it there.

He wrapped his fingers around hers with a smile. "Friends."

Hollee bumped her shoulder with his. "Are you ready for all of this?" She nodded at the room.

With her hair pulled back in a ponytail and almost no makeup on, she looked beautiful. There was no fear in her eyes, no hint of complaints about what they might find over the next couple of weeks. Instead, there was an eagerness in her demeanor that was contagious, even to someone as cynical as Clancy, who'd been in situations that had been shrouded in darkness and misery.

He tried to see things through her optimistic eyes. He felt old. Old and tired and not quite sure of his place in Arlington Regional, or in civilian life in general. He'd spent so much time in settings where everything had been so ultra-regimented that it was hard to adapt to some of his newfound freedoms. Maybe Bender, Virginia, would prove to be a bridge between those two worlds.

If so, he'd better make good use of his time, because he had a feeling these weeks would be over in the blink of an eye. Just like that night in Hollee's kitchen, when he'd felt the earth move beneath his feet. He still hadn't quite found his footing on it again.

Hollee had never been anywhere where people were treated in an actual barn, though the building hadn't housed animals in a very long time, instead holding the home owners' equipment, which had been sold when mining in the area had taken a downturn. And the hopelessness on the faces that lined the walls waiting their turns tugged at her heart. She worked as quickly as she could, but the crowd never seemed to thin.

By the third day she was more exhausted than she'd ever been in her life. To try to inject some tiny element of Christmas where there seemed to be none, she'd strung the Christmas lights in the small bedroom she shared with Kristen. But for the most part she was too tired to plug them in at night. Instead she fell into one of the twin beds feeling like she'd succeeded in moving a pebble up a very steep hill only to look behind her and see the landscape riddled with boulders, making her feeble efforts seem ludicrous. But they weren't. She had to believe that she—and the team before them—were making a difference.

Although many of the people they saw were poor, they cared for each other in a way that rivaled most families. And so everyone on their team owed it to them to do the best they could with what they had.

She'd barely seen Clancy, as she'd been dealing with pregnant women, and he'd been busy stitching up wounds and giving antibiotic and tetanus shots. Six o'clock found Hollee cleaning and sanitizing the exam room she'd been working in, since they were all taking turns with that chore. She was dead tired, but it was a good tired. She was wiping down the portable metal exam table when Clancy appeared in the doorway, dressed in jeans and a black shirt, holding some kind of tree in his hand. He looked like a lumberjack.

What in the world…?

She opened the door and ushered him in.

Not seeing him should have been a blessing, but instead… She'd missed him.

"Have you decided to take up gardening instead of medicine?"

He chuckled. "Not exactly. But since we're in the first week of December, I thought we should at least have a tree."

"A tree?"

Holding up his prize, he said, "Yep. Not an actual Christmas tree, since I couldn't find anything that I wouldn't need an ax to cut down, so I found a shrub instead."

It did have the look of an evergreen, but on a smaller scale, dirt still clinging to the roots. "I don't think anyone is going to realize it's a Christmas tree if there's nothing to go on it."

"That's where the fun comes in. I thought we could have the children come up with creative, free ways to decorate it. We could hold a contest, and the participants get one of the presents we brought in for sick kids. We could vote on a winner and give that child a bigger prize."

It was a wonderful idea. She shouldn't be surprised Clancy had thought up something like that. Not after witnessing the way he'd played the role of Santa. "I brought a small set of twinkle lights, but I think I've only turned them on once. Why don't we use them for this instead?" She smiled. "Where are we going to put it?"

"How about outside the entrance to the clinic, since more kids will be able to see it there? I've already gotten permission from Matt, the organizer."

She nodded. "I'm sure it's something they didn't give much thought to. We've been more worried about caring for people who are hurting."

"There's only so much we can do in a situation like this. It will take them a while to rebuild."

"Some of the moms are planning on moving to where they have other relatives, if they can talk their husbands into it. I think a tree will make everyone feel better, at least for the short term."

"I thought the same thing. Once you're done here, can you help me get it up and get the word out about the contest? Or are you too tired?"

A few minutes ago she would have said yes, but seeing him left her energized in a way she didn't want to analyze. "I'd love to help."

She looked at him with eyes that saw past the gorgeous package to the man beneath. A man she had always known was there, but it was as if she was seeing him again for the first time without the emotions from their past. She didn't know why he had done what he had, and she might never know, but surely people could change.

"Looks like that Santa costume rubbed off on you."

He gave a half shrug. "I enjoyed being him more than I thought I would. I figured with this…" He haphazardly motioned to the left side of his face. "…I'd be the last person they'd want in that suit."

A sharp twist of pain made her take a slow careful breath, blinking hard to keep her emotions in check. Maybe she wasn't the only one who was insecure about who they were. Her fears were the result of two men she'd loved turning their backs on her. And maybe his insecurities were rooted in a fear that his scars changed who he was.

"Clance, you have to know that those make no difference. To anyone."

They might to him, though, and she suspected there was a matching set of emotional scars that he carried inside him. And she was learning just how bitter a poison regret could be.

A question teetered on her tongue, and she was debating whether or not to ask him when he suddenly squeezed her hand and gave her a smile that warmed her to the core. "Thank you for that," he said.

The awful clawing sensation she'd had a moment earlier subsided as he continued. "Now, let's get this set up, so we can take a picture and put a flyer up on the door of the clinic."

Her idea about going back to being friends suddenly didn't seem quite so farfetched.

Unable to resist, she went up on tiptoe to kiss his cheek, startled when his index finger hooked under her chin. The quick impersonal touch she'd meant to give turned into something that was suddenly very personal as her lips touched his. She swallowed, her heart flipping a time or two, before she got it under control. Then they both pulled away and he gave her a glance that made her tingle all the way down to her toes.

She struggled to find her emotional balance, grabbing the first subject she could find, and hoping it would break the spell he'd cast over her.

"I think I know where we can put it," she murmured.

"Excuse me?"

His voice had a strangled quality that made her laugh. And just like that, the moment was over.

"I was talking about the tree. There's a five-gallon bucket we've been using as extra seating."

All of a sudden the door slammed open and a man who was soaking wet stood there holding a child.

"I need help! Randy fell in the river. I don't think he's breathing."

Clancy threw the tree to the side and grabbed the child from the man's arms. "I've got him."

He laid the boy, who couldn't have been more than five, facedown on the table, pushing firmly on his back to drain any lake water. A gush came out, then another. He flipped him back over, feeling his neck as he did. "Slight pulse, no respiration. Come on, Randy, don't do this."

He acted like he knew this boy.

Hollee dragged the crash cart around and placed an Ambu bag over the child's mouth, squeezing the bag to pump life-saving oxygen into his starved lungs. God, this town had had enough tragedy. She glanced at the man, who was shivering, his lips a dark shade of blue, a despair in his eyes that she'd seen before. He expected his son to die.

"Clance, can you take over for me for a second?"

He turned his head toward her, and when she nodded at the panic-stricken man, he nodded and moved to the boy's head.

Going to a small metal closet, she grabbed a blanket and draped it over the father's shoulders. The barn was heated, but it wasn't airtight and there was always a draft coming in. He'd obviously gone into the lake after the boy and with the frigid temperatures outside, he was in danger of hypothermia.

The man started to shake his head and drop the cover behind him, but she grabbed it and looked him in the face. "Take it. We don't need two patients."

That must have convinced him because he wrapped the blanket around himself.

"What's your name?" she asked.

"Samuel."

"Do you know how long Randy was in the water, Samuel?"

"I don't know. Maybe ten minutes. He was playing, gathering some twigs for my sister's fireplace, while I went back to get the fish we'd caught. When I glanced over, he was in the water, the current carrying him down-river. He looked so scared. So very scared." His voice caught, and he dragged a hand through his wet hair. "God, how could I have left him alone? I've already lost my wife and daughter. I can't lose Randy."

Her heart squeezed so hard it threatened to paralyze her. But she knew better than let it take control.

"You found him. Got him out of the water. That's what counts." She hesitated. "Let me go help him."

She went back over to Clancy, her lungs catching for a second when she saw he was no longer working the mechanical respirator. Instead, he had his stethoscope out, listening to his chest. "He's breathing on his own."

Never had she heard five more beautiful words. "His heart?"

"Believe it or not, it's strong. But I'm going to have him transported to Richland to be monitored for edema."

Sometimes, after a drowning victim had been revived, irritation and inflammation could cause the lungs to fill with fluid, a secondary complication that could be almost as deadly as the original event.

"I agree." She lowered her voice. "Do you know them?"

"I talked to them right after we got off the bus." He looked at her. "They've lost everything, Hollee."

"I know. He told me." She glanced back at the dad. "He said Randy was in the water for about ten minutes. In this case the frigid water probably helped slow tissue damage."

"My thoughts too."

The boy sputtered and opened his eyes, coughing for several seconds before trying to sit up. Hollee put a hand on his shoulder. "It's okay, Randy. Your dad is right here." She turned and motioned him over.

When the man reached the table, he practically fell onto it as he gathered his son in his arms, the blanket falling to the ground unheeded. As rough and tough as this man looked, his eyes told another story. "I don't know how to thank you."

Hollee draped the blanket back over him. "You just did." It was true. Not very long ago she'd wondered if she was making a difference. Here was proof that she was. That Clancy was. That everyone who came through this town, hoping to do some good, was doing exactly that.

"I'm going to arrange transport," Clancy said. They'd been flying critical patients out, but since Randy was stable for the moment, he'd probably be taken by car to the other hospital.

Within fifteen minutes, a woman brought Randy and his dad some dry clothes and coats, then she hugged the pair for a long time. The sister he'd talked about?

Randy was well enough to wave at them as he was carried to a waiting car.

Matt, their liaison from FEMA, saw the pair off and then turned to her and Clancy. "Looks like you two have had some excitement this afternoon." He nodded at the tree lying in the corner. "And I'm taking it that

that's going to be the Christmas tree we talked about?"

"It is."

Randy hadn't been the only excitement. It was a good thing the man hadn't walked in on their kiss or they might have been shipped home.

Why? Surely they'd had husband and wife teams here before. Except she and Clancy weren't husband and wife. And she certainly didn't want Kristen or anyone else from the hospital to get wind of what had happened in that exam room. It would give that picture of them in the newsletter a whole different connotation. And put paid to the idea that they didn't know each other well.

The fact was they knew each other all too well.

Matt headed back out, and an hour later, they'd planted their little tree in the bucket which they'd then wrapped with a canvas tarp. With a bit of artful folding and tucking, it made a passable tree stand, especially after winding a red strip of elastic bandaging around it and tying the ends in a bow.

They then watered it and set it just outside the door. "All we need now are your lights.

Are you sure you're okay with us using them? You probably won't get them back."

"I'm sure. I knew there was a reason I wanted them so badly."

He put his hands on his hips, fingers loosely perched on the lean bones in a way that made her mouth water. "Matt said we can invite the town's kids and have a tree-lighting ceremony tomorrow night."

Right now she would have agreed with almost anything he suggested. Not that it wasn't a good idea. It was. And a little burst of excitement washed away the tiredness she'd felt just an hour earlier.

"The kids are going to love it." Maybe every volunteer group did something to help celebrate the holidays, and maybe this was as much about giving this town a shot of hope as it was anything else. But whatever it was, they were about to add a little bit of fun to their last week and a half in Bender, and maybe leave a little piece of themselves behind in the process.

CHAPTER EIGHT

AT DUSK THE next day, a crowd of around a hundred people stood around the barn's entrance. Hollee had agreed with Clancy that it was best to put the tree just outside the door. That way, all the children who made decorations could walk by and see it. It wasn't a huge tree, but at almost five feet tall, it was big enough to fit a fair number of decorations. And the tree would carry a piece of many of Bender's residents. It was another way to bring people together.

The rest of the staff loved the idea and were as excited as Hollee seemed to be. One of them had run to the nearest town and purchased a couple more strands of lights to add to Hollee's. But they'd agreed that all the other decorations would be handmade by the children and their families.

Matt addressed the group. "Are you ready for Bender's official Christmas tree lighting ceremony?"

"Ready!" The voices sounded in chorus, with some of the children clapping in excitement.

Clancy held the plug for the lights and waited for the other man to give the signal, very aware Hollee was standing off to the side. He didn't want her way over there. He wanted her next to him, and that bothered him more than he cared to admit.

Because of that shared moment yesterday?

Randy was there in the front row along with his father, having been released from the hospital after a night of observation. They'd gotten back to Bender just an hour ago, just in time for the tree lighting. He'd been horrified when Samuel had carried his limp form into the hospital. The outcome could have been very different. Seeing him well enough to join in the festivities made him glance at Hollee, who nodded as if to say she'd noticed the pair.

Matt looked at him with a smile. "Let's do it, then."

In addition to being a FEMA doctor, Matt would be here for most of the rebuilding and to help direct future volunteer teams as they worked toward that goal so Clancy could always write and ask for updates or maybe even come back at a later date and help again.

Clancy plugged in the lights and the tree sprang to life. Three strands might have been a little overkill, but they did the job, sending a message to everyone that the season was about more than just a man in a red suit.

An "Ooh" went up from those who were in attendance. The multitude of colorful bulbs stood out in stark contrast to the darkening skies.

Too many lights or not, all he wanted was for this to bring a tiny bit of magic to these kids. Especially after what they'd gone through. How many children, like Randy, had lost members of their families? He couldn't begin to imagine.

Matt had asked Clancy to explain what they wanted to do. So he asked the kids to get ready to use their imaginations.

"This tree needs decorations. Lots of

them. But we don't want to buy them. We want you to make them." He paused to let that sink in. "So figure out something that you can draw or construct, using your own two hands. You can use materials you find around town. Recycled items would be even better. Don't worry about how to hang your decorations on the tree, just bring them in, and we'll figure that out."

When several voices started talking all at once, he knew they'd done what they'd hoped to do: put a tiny bit of excitement back in the season.

He raised his hand to quiet the crowd for a moment. "Bring your projects back on Wednesday—that's a week from today—and we'll put them on the tree. Everyone who participates will get a little gift, and the most imaginative creation will pick a prize donated from our hospital in Arlington."

Matt spoke up. "We're also going to have a Christmas party for everyone in the main part of the barn afterward. Those who can, bring a dish of finger foods to share. Those who can't, come anyway."

The level of excitement rose, and Clancy smiled, glancing over at Hollee to see that she too was smiling. She gave him a quick thumbs-up sign, which made him swallow.

She'd talked about being friends, and yet when she'd gone to kiss him on the cheek he hadn't been able to leave it at that. Damn. What was it about this woman that made him go sideways? Every time?

He'd toyed with telling her the truth about Jacob and seeing if that made it stop. But the time for that was long past. Why not let her go on thinking her husband had been a saint?

He hated it. Because it turned out that his old friend had been anything but. But this wasn't about him. Or about Jacob and his failings. It was about not hurting Hollee.

People filed through and shook their hands, thanking them for coming and for what they were doing, some of the kids already picking up twigs and tree limbs.

Hollee came over to him. "This was a great idea. Did you see Randy's face?"

"I did. It's good to see him back so soon."

She wrapped her jacket around herself. "Yes, it is."

"I like the idea of giving gifts out to the children who bring in ornaments."

"I don't think we have enough presents for every single child in town, even though the hospital added some useful items before we left, like fun cups and socks, et cetera. But it was the only way I could think of to make it fair."

A lot in life was unfair and right now he was suddenly peering through the fog of the last ten years and wondering if he'd done the right thing. If he'd not stepped aside for Jacob, would he and Hollee have wound up together?

Hell, what damn good did it do to rehash this again and again? He and Hollee were not together. And from what she'd said after that incident in her kitchen, she still loved Jacob. He was who she'd chosen to be with, so the jerk had evidently been right. Clancy hadn't deserved Hollee back then. But from what he'd seen at that hotel in Afghanistan, neither had Jacob.

Working with her here in Bender was proving to be an exercise in torture. He was dreaming about her at night and working with her during the day. A lethal combination.

Kristen came over to talk to Hollee, and

he gratefully took that as his cue to leave.
And that was fine with him, since he could
use a nice cold beer. Or two or three. Bender
had instituted a three-drink maximum at the
local bar, partly to conserve their supplies
and partly to keep the residents from trying
to drown their troubles with booze.

Well, he wasn't trying to drown his troubles—plural—he was only trying to drown
out one particular trouble. And that trouble
had started the moment they'd begun working together.

Clancy had seemed off for the last several
days, but she couldn't put her finger on exactly how. He'd been friendly enough, but
there was an emotional detachment that
hadn't been there earlier in the week. And
certainly there'd been no more touching moments like they'd shared in that exam room,
when his light kiss had lit her up as brightly
as the Christmas tree standing outside the
door.

She shifted her instrument tray, not used
to playing surgical nurse, even though she'd
done a rotation in it during her training. But
the regular nurse was sick with a stomach

bug and Matt had asked if she'd fill in, since there were no active labor cases right now. She'd seen Clancy's eyes when she'd stepped into the room. There had been a combination of dismay and resignation in them that had made her throat tighten.

He didn't like working with her, despite his assurances that they could be friends.

Maybe she'd been fooling herself. Two nights ago, he'd come up to her, and she could have sworn he'd had something on his mind, something he'd wanted to say, but in the end he'd just discussed the tree and ordinary things about the town and then left as quickly as he'd appeared.

It had been more surreal than the kiss they'd shared in the exam room.

"Suture."

She handed him the needle threaded with the suture material, bringing her mind back to the task at hand. Three-year-old Kaley was lying sedated on the table. The little girl had fallen while holding a glass of water and had cut her lip right through the vermillion border. They'd called in Clancy, since an error in lining up the edges would be noticeable as the girl got older. Strapping the child to a papoose board had quickly proved to be a no-go. The panicked child had screamed helplessly, causing her parents almost as much distress as it did Kaley.

Clancy had loosened the restraints himself, making soothing sounds as he carried the toddler over to her mom, and then asked the anesthesiologist to prepare a light sedation instead of physically restraining the child. It worked like a charm and soon Kaley was out like a light.

The sight of him holding that little girl had almost been her undoing. Just like seeing him with his niece, and later with Randy. He was so amazingly gentle with children. If he ever found the right woman, maybe he'd...

What? Settle down?

She didn't see that happening, and what Clancy did or didn't do was none of her business.

Four minutes later he'd finished the top lip and everything lined up perfectly.

Unfortunately the same couldn't be said of her dealings with Clancy, where nothing seemed to line up and where she was busy playing a psychological version of the mix-up-the-cups game. She was never sure which emotion was hidden under which cup at any given time. Pick up the wrong cup and—*oops!*—there it would be, on display for everyone to see. Like in that Santa picture.

She didn't need any more slipups like that one.

"Okay, moving to the lower lip." He glanced at her, his attention dipping to her mouth before tugging his loupes down and shielding his eyes from view. Maybe she wasn't the only one slipping up.

"Can you rinse the area again, please?

Okay, his brusque tone said she'd imagined that look. His mind, unlike hers, was completely focused on his job.

Using the bottle of saline, she washed the blood from the area, granting Clancy a clear view of what he had to work with.

Should she do the same thing? Sluice some emotional saline and just come out and ask Clancy if something was bothering him? What if he gave her the standard "nothing's wrong" reply?

She couldn't force him to talk. And she wasn't really sure she wanted to know, especially if it went back to what had happened between them in her kitchen.

No, he'd seemed to put that behind him a lot easier than she had. Except he'd kissed her again in that exam room. And he had seemed to glance at her lips a few seconds ago.

Was Clancy really as indifferent as he seemed at this moment?

She didn't know. And she wasn't sure she wanted to know. She had time. There was still a little over a week before they had to leave Bender. Surely before then she could figure this thing out. And then she could go back to Arlington with an assurance that she knew exactly where he stood.

A week later, she was no closer to knowing where they stood than she'd been during Kaley's surgery, and time was up. It was decorating day. The crowds that had swamped their little clinic each day had again assembled outside the barn. But tonight it was for a different reason. And despite her uncertainties, the town's excitement was infectious. This was probably the first fun thing they'd done as a community since the disaster. Kids were chattering in animated voices, holding their offerings for the tree.

She allowed the turmoil and tension from working with Clancy to be washed to one side, at least for tonight.

Except he was the official MC for the event, since this had been his idea. She stood next to a large box that contained the gifts she would hand out to the kids who participated. There was also a pair of scissors and suture material that they would use to hang the ornaments. The tree was already lit, its glow like a beacon that made the crowd gather closer, their coats and gloves helping to keep the December chill at bay.

Clancy picked up the microphone, sending a long glance her way before turning back to the group in front of them.

Her heart tripped before righting itself.

Get a hold of yourself, Hollee.

That was hard to do when the man was heartbreakingly gorgeous. He always had been, that slight bad-boy air he'd carried with him as a teenager was still as potent as any pharmaceutical known to man. No wonder he'd had women swarming over him back then, her included. Even those scars did nothing to diminish his looks, as evidenced by the woman who'd slipped him that piece of paper at the dog park. Even here, he'd gotten sideways glances from some of the nurses, Kristen included, who'd asked if there was something between her and Clancy.

She'd flatly denied it. Did that mean Kristen was going to set her sights on him?

"I think we're ready to start," he said. "Who wants to be first?" He gestured at the lit but still empty tree.

Two kids moved forward—the resemblance between them unmistakable. They held matching stars made out of twigs that had been wired together.

Hollee peeled off her mittens and fashioned loops out of the suture material, before handing the ornaments back to the brothers and letting them choose where to put them. "Good job, you guys." She gave each of them a wrapped gift.

One by one they presented their treasures to Hollee for loops. The ornaments ranged from pictures scratched on bits of paper to a tiny wooden box that contained a nativity scene made from pebbles.

Very imaginative.

Another child had found a clear plastic soda bottle and cut what looked like icicles from it. There were twenty or so of them.

As things got more congested, Kristen came up to help her make hanging loops.

"Clancy came up with a great idea. I've never seen a more beautiful tree."

She hadn't either, and a sudden squeezing in her throat caught her by surprise.

"It's perfect." And it was. This dug-up-from-the-earth impromptu Christmas tree was somehow more special than all the trees at the hospital, or even the trees she and Jacob had shared over the years. The fear that its specialness had something to do with the man who'd spearheaded this event made her hands ball up at her sides.

She'd seen so many different sides of Clancy during this trip. Things that she'd never thought about or looked for when they had been younger. Like the way he'd taken Randy from his dad's arms—the intensity and determination behind his gaze making her believe that everything was going to be okay. Or the way he'd held his sister's baby with such tenderness. Or how he'd set up a tree for a struggling, heartbroken community and given them hope.

Dwelling on any of that right now was sure to turn her into a giant waterworks, so those thoughts would have to wait until she knew she wouldn't dissolve. Until then, she needed to hold it together.

It had to be the highs and lows of the last two weeks kicking in. It had nothing to do with Clancy, or what they'd been through. At least she hoped not. Because when they got back to Arlington things would return to normal. In every way.

So she sent her friend a smile. "Who is your pick for best decoration?"

"Those icicles are really cool." She glanced at where the maker was still hanging them on the tree. With each slight breeze, they twirled and sparkled, catching the light from the tree and magnifying it. "It's amazing what they came up with, and a good lesson for us all that keeping things simple is sometimes best."

"Yes, it is." She could apply that lesson to her current situation. She needed to keep things with Clancy simple and stop letting her feelings and emotions from the past bleed into the present.

Remember that fortune, Hollee. The past belongs to the past.

The icicles were up, and it looked like that might be all the ornaments. Then Randy's dad led him to the front of the crowd and gave him an encouraging nudge. He looked healthy but shy, hesitantly coming forward carrying something in a plastic bag.

Clancy looked inside, and his head cocked for a second as if puzzled. Then his throat moved with a quick jerk and he motioned for the child's dad to come up. Wearing worn jeans and a T-shirt sporting the name of the state football team, the bearded man moved toward them, draping his arm around his son.

"Hi, Randy." Clancy gave the child a smile. "Let's see what you brought for our tree."

Hollee's heart squeezed, that weepy sensation growing stronger. Maybe she'd fall apart after all.

Clancy pulled out a length of red yarn. Strung along it were bead-like items. Some were silver and shiny, and some were a dark dull color, almost like rust or—

"Oh, wow," Kristen said.

The words made her take a closer look, then she realized the part of the garland that was visible contained pieces of hardware. Odds and ends. Hinges and nuts and bolts and even a silver doorknob. Her chest tightened.

Clancy spoke into the microphone before holding it in front of the man's mouth. "I'd like you to tell us the story behind these items, if you don't mind."

The man took off his hat and nodded. "I didn't want the kids to step on nails after the tornado, so I borrowed a metal detector and started going through the streets and properties where..." He took a deep breath before continuing. "Where some of our houses used to be. I put them in a bucket, intending to throw them away. One bucket became two, and two became three. I realized these things were once part of this town and could be again." He rubbed a hand over his head. "They'd be a great way to remember what happened, to remember our loved ones. So I'm going to use them to rebuild my house. To rebuild my neighbors' houses. When the call came for items to put on the tree, Randy asked if he could use some of the stuff from the buckets."

He nodded at the bag. "These are what he chose."

The squeezing in her chest grew fiercer, and when she looked out over the townspeople she didn't see a dry eye out there. Some people were openly sobbing, including Randy's aunt and her family.

Clancy reached out and gripped the other man's hand, giving it a firm shake. "I can't think of a better thing to put on this tree. A tree that belongs to the people of Bender, Virginia. Will you both help me loop it around?"

Putting down his microphone, there was an almost reverent silence as Randy, his dad and Clancy wrapped the garland around the tree, carefully tucking it beneath the icicles and other ornaments, the gathered items a bittersweet reminder of what they'd lost, but also a picture of hope. These things would eventually be put back to use, showing that what had happened in the past could merge into the future, that it wasn't entirely lost.

Hadn't she just been thinking about that fortune and her past with Clancy? And how it had nothing to do with the present? What if she was wrong?

The garland was on, and Randy and his dad rejoined the rest of the townsfolk. Several clapped the father on the back and gave his son a quick squeeze. Others took pictures of the tree with their phones. As Hollee gazed at it, she realized Kristen was right. She'd likely never see a tree like it again in her life.

"Is that everyone?" Clancy's voice startled her, and she couldn't stop the shudder that rolled through her at the words. At the thought of never seeing him breathe life into another child. Or having him hook a finger under her chin to tip her face up for his kiss. Once they were back home, it would be all over. They would go their own separate ways. Yes, they might see each other for Jen-Jen's christening or around the hospital. But...

Was that all?

It's only been a little over a month since he came back to Arlington, Hollee. You can't get attached that fast.

Maybe not, but what about over the space of ten years?

"If we have all the decorations, we're going to ask our panel of judges to pick a winner, but first let me say that this tree wouldn't be what it is without *all* of your contributions. I never expected such a variety of creative ideas. You've made something special out of what was once a scraggly old tree." He smiled and glanced around the group. "I hope you'll remember this as you grow up. It doesn't matter what you have as much as it matters what you *make* out of what you have. Randy's garland is a great reminder of that."

And sometimes you had something beautiful and didn't make anything out of it at all. Even her life with Jacob had turned out differently from what she had thought it would be. What it might have been.

One of the hospital staff members took several more photos of the tree from various angles, probably for Arlington Regional's newsletter.

Mixed in with the furor of other emotions was a hint of sadness over leaving this quaint mining town behind. The trip had been about caring and helping and… loving. She wished there was some way to stay in contact with Randy and some of the other folks she'd met over the past couple of weeks.

Maybe she could come back someday. Why not?

Clancy formed a huddle with the others on the voting panel, one of whom was Kristen, who'd excused herself to be with them.

Hollee was glad she wasn't on it. She could just enjoy the tree and not have to worry about that uncasy awareness that crept in whenever she stood too close to him.

Who was she kidding? All she had to do was lay eyes on the man and her traitorous pulse picked up its pace.

Five minutes later, Clancy stepped forward. "We've reached a decision. Randy, would you come up here, please?"

Hollee pulled in a quick breath, needing the shot of oxygen.

The little boy glanced up at his dad, who nodded. He hurried over to them, stopping beside Clancy, who put his hand on the child's shoulder. "I heard something else about you. Can you tell me if it's true? Someone told me that you're actually helping your dad collect some of the items that are on your garland, and that you spent most of the night stringing it." Randy nodded and Clancy looked up at everyone. "When you get a chance, you should come by and look at it."

Clancy knelt beside the boy while Kristen handed him a wrapped box. "We want to give you this to remember us by."

Randy took the present, fingering the stick-on bow. "Can I open it?"

"Yes, of course."

The little boy carefully peeled away the bow and paper and inside was a flat white gift box. Opening it, Randy's eyes got huge, and he looked up at Clancy. "This is mine?"

He nodded, picking up a white stethoscope. "Yep. Let me show you how to listen to your heart." He put the earpieces in the boy's ears and then held it to his chest. "Can you hear it?"

His head bobbed a couple of times and a huge smile appeared on his face.

"I used this same stethoscope to listen to your heart after your accident. You'll never know how glad I was to hear that strong beat thumping away in your chest."

Clancy removed the earbuds and draped

the item around Randy's neck with a smile. Soon the boy was engulfed by his friends, the Christmas tree forgotten as everyone waited their turn to listen to each other's hearts.

Wait a minute. That was the 'scope he'd used on Randy? She swallowed. Tomorrow was their last full day in Bender, and Clancy had just given away his personal stethoscope—which were normally closely guarded by their owners. He was leaving a tangible piece of himself with the boy he'd helped save. With the town he'd poured his life into over the last two weeks.

And that's when she realized Clancy had poured a part of himself into her heart as well, whether he'd meant to or not.

She loved him. Loved his selflessness and caring nature, even when he appeared to be at his most unapproachable. Loved everything she'd learned about him during their time in Bender.

Only there was nothing she could do about it. Not ten years ago, and certainly not now.

Not without risking her heart all over again.

* * *

Some of the partitions in the barn had been pushed back to allow room for a festive group of tables to be set up. People from both the Arlington volunteer team and the town had come together to make a wonderful spread of finger foods and drinks, careful to make sure that anything alcoholic was kept well out of reach of the kids. The three-drink maximum had been lifted for this one night, but Clancy doubted anyone would tiptoe over that line. Especially not tonight.

Clancy couldn't believe how fast time had flown. Soon they would be back in Arlington, far from the sights and sounds of what had happened in this town. And, truth be told, he'd miss it. He'd miss seeing the rebuilding process, especially seeing where the bits and pieces of recycled hardware from Randy's garland would wind up.

It was the first field hospital he'd worked in as a civilian, and the focus was so totally different from the military as to be like night and day. This was all about helping rather than defending, although he'd done his share of helping while in the army. But there was a freedom to come and go and decide things for oneself, within certain parameters. They still had to work as a team, but it wasn't as regimented as he was used to. Kind of like life at Arlington Regional.

He'd found Hollee standing by herself and went over to join her. There was laughter and music was playing, but it wasn't being blasted out of speakers.

Kristen came by before he'd said a word. "We kept the center clear for anyone who wants to do some...dancing." She said that last word in a sing-song voice, nudging Hollee's arm and grinning when her friend flashed her an acid glare.

Great. Dancing. He glanced around the room, wondering if Hollee would partner with any of the team.

It's none of your business, Clancy.

And it wasn't. But that didn't mean that he could just shut his brain off whenever it veered in the wrong direction. And this was definitely the wrong direction. Because he found himself wanting to be the one to dance with her. Despite trying to avoid her for the last week.

But it was the last night. Surely he could pass it off as something unimportant.

Like he had ten years ago? Not something he wanted to think about tonight.

The music went up a couple of notches, and some of the children and others headed onto the floor and started moving to the beat. At least this wasn't the stuff slow dances were made of.

He realized Hollee was still standing next to him. "Do you two want something to drink?"

Kristen shook her head. "Nothing for me, I'm headed out onto the floor in a minute."

"I'd love a glass of soda or even a beer if there's some up there," Hollee said. "Thank you."

He headed to the table just as Kristen tugged one of Hollee's hands. "Come on. It'll be fun. There aren't enough men to go around. Besides, most everyone in our group is married except a couple of the doctors, us and a few other nurses."

Hollee tried to resist for a second, but when her friend persisted, she gave a quick shrug, and then went out and started danc-ing. Clancy tensed, his instinct to stop and watch her whispering in his ear. He already knew he loved the way she moved but that was a temptation he should definitely resist. Even so, as he waited in line for his turn at the drinks table, he turned and glanced over. She was laughing at something Kristen had said, clapping her hand over her mouth for a moment, hiding that little dimple that he knew was there.

He'd already had a few moments of weakness when it came to her. To continue down that path might prove disastrous, especially with all the messiness that had happened with Jacob. She might not know about it, but if he tried to build a relationship with her, knowing he was keeping that a secret, he'd have a hard time living with himself. And he really didn't want to be the one to tell her.

Why couldn't you have done what you promised, Jacob?

Impulsive acts brought…complications. He'd found that out, and so had his former friend.

By the time he got back with their drinks, Hollee had changed partners. She was now dancing with…

One of the doctors. A man this time. He was assuming it was one of the single ones Kristen had mentioned.

And the man's gaze was as steady as a cobra's, poised to strike.

"Well, damn." The oath was enough to make someone at a nearby table glance at him.

You are crazy, Clancy. These are team members. No one is throwing cobra looks at anyone.

Holly wasn't dating. She'd said it herself, she hadn't slept with anyone since Jacob.

His teeth clenched at that thought. His friend had been dead for five years. Why *hadn't* Hollce gotten married again?

Because she was mourning him? Still? Or because she just hadn't found the right person?

Like this doctor?

He felt like a fool, standing there holding two glasses, so he went over to one of the tables and sat, putting one glass in front of the chair next to his. Then he took a long drink of his beer. At least tonight he didn't have to worry about driving. Not that he planned on getting drunk or anything.

The other man touched Holly from time to time. Subtle gestures. Fingers to fingers, a palm on her arm. She appeared to take a step back at that, only to have the man slowly close the gap, making the move appear casual. He wasn't right on top of her by any stretch of the imagination but even so, a warning pressure began to build in Clancy's head.

He swallowed another drink of his beer. Kristen rejoined the pair, and a feeling of relief swept through him when Hollee seemed to glance at her friend gratefully, again laughing at something she said, while the other man didn't seem at all happy with the interruption.

What the hell was he doing sitting here, brooding in silence? He'd never been a man to sit back and ignore something he didn't like.

Like Jacob moving in on Hollee?

That had been different. Jacob had given him a pretty bitter pill to swallow, but it had also made him take a look at himself and decide to make a change.

Clancy was no longer the person he'd been back then. Did he deserve Hollee?

Maybe not. But a single dance? That was a different story.

Taking one more bracing gulp, he climbed to his feet, leaving their glasses where they were. His initial goal was to tell her that her drink was ready. That goal shifted when the music changed, a much slower Christmas song thrumming through the speakers. Since most of these people were either colleagues or residents of Bender with a healthy sprinkling of children throughout, there probably wouldn't be a whole lot of slow dancing, and for that he was grateful. Because all he wanted to do was to draw Hollee into his arms, feel her skin against his, breathe her scent deep into his lungs. Even though it was a recipe for disaster.

Dancing with her. Standing across from her and letting the wistful tune carry them both away.

He made it across the floor, and as soon as he faced Hollee he saw her smile. Not just something polite that welcomed him to their little group but a genuine smile that warmed her eyes in a way that caused his lips to tilt upward.

"I knew I'd get you out here sooner or later," she said.

He blinked in surprise, until the other man excused himself. Then he realized why she'd said it. So he hadn't imagined her discomfort. Kristen leaned in and kissed Hollee's cheek, murmuring, "I had a feeling... Don't worry, I don't think you need saving from this one."

Then she, too, left.

"Sorry," Clancy murmured. "I wasn't sure if you were enjoying yourself, but I wanted to tell you that I have our drinks at one of the tables."

"I wasn't. Enjoying myself." Her eyes met his in a way that told him exactly what she meant. She hadn't liked dancing with that guy. And he was glad. Fiercely glad.

"It looks like you have a good friend in Kristen, then."

"Yes. She's been there for me, even when things got..."

"Got?"

"Complicated."

That made him frown, since it was the same word that had flashed across his brain a few minutes ago. How long had she known Kristen?

"As in with Jacob?"

"Kind of." She shrugged. "I wanted to start a family, but that didn't...happen."

Because she couldn't? Or because Jacob had been against it? If he had been so consumed with other women, why hadn't he just divorced Hollee? An ugly thought came to him that he quickly discarded.

He and Jacob had always been competitive, but he'd never told his friend about the kiss he and Hollee had shared. And there was no way Jacob would have risked her happiness out of selfish ego. Would he?

But he'd always believed Hollee was deeply in love with her husband.

"I'm sorry that didn't work out for you. You would make a great mother." He paused trying to figure out how to word it. "You still could be one. There's always adoption. Or you might meet someone else."

"I don't know. I've given that some thought. But I'm so busy that I barely have time for Tommie, much less a baby. And I definitely wouldn't have had time to come on this trip if I had a young child."

"I'm glad you did."

"Excuse me?"

"I'm glad you came." Surprisingly enough, it was true.

Her pupils widened. "You are? Because you didn't seem all that thrilled that I was coming when you saw me in the conference room."

"I could say the same about you. Chalk it up to surprise, in my case." Which was also true.

And now here he was dancing with her. Smart move? Probably not. But better than letting that doc keep hitting on her, especially since she'd said she hadn't liked it.

A few minutes later the FEMA liaison tapped them on the shoulder. "How much have you had to drink?"

"Nothing," Hollee said.

Clancy blinked. What the hell? There was no way the man thought he was drunk. "Just part of a beer, why?"

"We've got a situation and several of us have already had more than our share."

Immediately on alert, he said, "What is it?"

"One of the residents in an outlying area

is in labor. The roads are washed out and the midwife has run into trouble. She sent one of the kids to get help."

"God." Hollee's distress wasn't lost on him.

"Well, the kid made it here somehow. Have you got something that can get through?"

"Several of the residents have four-wheel-drive vehicles, but anything heavy is going to get bogged down in the mud. We already tried to get back into those areas last week."

"How did the kid get here?"

"He came on an ATV."

"If you can get me some directions and keep him safe, I'll get my gear together and borrow it."

"I'm going too," Holly said. "I've ridden on your bike with you. You know I can do it."

He did. He remembered a couple of times that he'd had her behind him as they'd torn up some of the local fields. And then there was the night he'd kissed her.

"It's going to be cold going."

She frowned, her chin tilting up. "We don't have time to argue. This is what I'm trained for. Besides, you gave away your stethoscope. You'll need mine…and me."

Yes, he would. And he was beginning to think he needed her in more ways than one. "Okay, you grab a coat and I'll get my medical kit."

The ATV was one of the bigger ones, the wheels set wide apart and looking good and sturdy. It was also splattered with mud, attesting to the fact that it was going to be rough going.

"I'm going to need you to navigate," he said as they buckled on helmets borrowed from other Bender residents.

"Okay. My phone's GPS is working, so I'm going to try to use that as much as possible, but I have written instructions in my back pocket as well."

"Perfect." He climbed on, waiting for her to get on behind him. The slope of the seat tipped her tight against him, which was probably a good thing, even though it reminded him of the past and did a number on his head. "Hang on."

Soon they were off, the frigid wind whistling past them. A pothole threatened to rattle his teeth out of his head, but that would soon be the least of their worries once the pavement gave out. Which it did about five miles out of town.

He slowed down, the tracks from the kid's flight into town plainly visible. "I see his path. Here we go." He eased the vehicle down into the mud.

Things got hairy for a while and maneuvering through the worst of the muck had them shimmying sideways a time or two. Hollee's arms squeezed his midsection in a death grip. He could remember a time when he might have chosen the worst spots for just that reason. Today was not one of them.

One of her arms left him. "Stop for just a second."

He immediately throttled down. "What is it?"

"Checking distance. We're about a mile out."

He again wondered about the wisdom of her coming, rather than leaving her to finish enjoying the party, but she was right. He would need her. Although he had delivered babies before, it wasn't his specialty, and Hollee had assisted with lots of them.

The last mile went quickly, and they pulled up outside a small bungalow-style log home. Clancy laid on the horn to let them know they were there before they both leaped off the vehicle. The front door opened in a rush and a man stood there.

"Thank God you're here! Please, hurry. The baby is…stuck."

His heart turned to ice, and when he looked at Hollee he saw that she'd gone pale.

"Not good," she whispered.

She wasn't kidding. He cast around for the training he'd had on shoulder dystocia, as he assumed that's what the man had meant by being "stuck." A wedged shoulder was a medical emergency, because once the baby's head was delivered, the rest of the body needed to follow quickly.

Clancy quickly introduced them to the man. "The midwife's with her?"

"Yes."

They were in the bedroom in a matter of seconds, asking her husband to wait outside. The midwife was calling out instructions, telling the young woman on the bed not to push, even as she attempted to reposition her legs and hips.

Clancy assessed the situation, communicating with the birthing assistant. "What's the status?"

"The baby's shoulder is wedged. I've tried everything short of attempting to push it back in and do a C-section—which I wouldn't, of course," she added quickly, "but I can't get anywhere."

Pushing the baby back in was a last-ditch measure and dangerous for both the mother and unborn child.

Hollee touched his arm. "We need to go through the maneuvers in order. We can help you with them." She glanced at the midwife and got a nod in response.

"I live just down the road. There's no way we could have gotten her to a hospital and there's nowhere to land a chopper back here."

"Yeah, I can see that. It's bad out there."

Clancy shed his coat and went into a nearby bathroom to sluice his hands with soap and water, Hollee appearing beside him to do the same.

With the midwife's help they positioned the woman so her knees were pressed to her chest. Then while Hollee put pressure on the patient's abdomen just above the pubic bone, Clancy attempted gentle rotation, hoping to free the shoulder. The woman's agonized cries tore at him, but there was no access to an epidural or other pain medication, and if they didn't get this resolved quickly, they were in danger of losing both mom and baby.

The baby rotated partially, but the shoulder didn't budge. "Dammit. I really don't want to perform a cleidotomy." The drastic measure involved a deliberate fracture of the baby's collarbone in the hope that the shoulder would then fit through the pelvis.

Hollee looked him in the eye. "We're going to do whatever it takes, Clancy. Whatever. It. Takes. But let's try the corkscrew first."

The midwife nodded her agreement. From the look of them, both the birthing professional and laboring mom were exhausted. If this failed, the next step was to get her up on all fours. But he doubted the young mother had the strength to hold herself up at this point.

"Ready?" he asked.

Hollee nodded, and when he directed a

look at the midwife, she anticipated their every move.

This had better work. They were running out of options. Clancy slowly rotated the baby's head once again, being more aggressive about it this time, while Hollee located the baby's shoulder and pushed down hard, trying to dislodge it from beneath the bone. It stuck tight for a terrible few seconds, even as Clancy continued the rotation, then suddenly something popped and shifted. "I think we may be free."

"I think so too."

"Okay, let's push. But without a lot of force." He added the warning, needing this to be a controlled slide otherwise the baby might end up wedged all over again.

The mom bore down, and the first shoulder appeared in the birth canal. Damn, it had worked.

"Keep pushing, you can do it!" he said. "One, two, three..." The midwife took up the count, guiding the process from her place at the woman's head. The look of relief on her face was unmistakable.

Two more pushes and, unbelievably, the baby slid onto the readied towel as if there had never been an issue. Carefully cradling the newborn, praying they'd won the race against time, he said, "It's a girl."

The baby's legs kicked, and then she squinched up her face as if registering her extreme displeasure with what had just transpired. He smiled, while rubbing her briskly with the towel to stimulate her, gratified to hear her sudden angry howl. "Sorry about all of that, sweetheart. You gave us quite a scare."

"Thank God. You did it, Maria." The midwife dropped a kiss on the woman's cheek. The new mom must have realized it was going to be okay, because she started weeping, her body going slack.

The midwife brought over surgical scissors, waiting until the cord had stopped pulsing. Then she clamped and cut it.

Hollee came over. "If you'll check her clavicle and make she wasn't injured in the maneuver, I'll make sure there's no postpartum hemorrhage as we deliver the placenta."

He'd just been about to do that. Once he was satisfied the newborn's respiratory system was working well, he laid her on the bed and ran careful fingers along the clavicle and humerus on the affected side. No breaks. He breathed a word of thanks.

She was perfect. Absolutely perfect. The baby had stopped crying, her big blue eyes struggling to focus on him.

"Hi, there, beautiful. You have no idea how happy I am to see you."

"So am I." Hollee was back beside him, her shoulder brushing his as she looked down at the baby. "She is beautiful. Rita— our midwife—has everything under control. I imagine she's dealt with things like this before, but sometimes it all happens so fast, and when you don't have an extra set of hands when you need them...well, it can get overwhelming."

"Yes, it can. Speaking of which, thanks for walking me through things. It's been a while."

"You did a wonderful job and delivered a healthy baby. That's all that counts in the end."

He smiled and touched a finger to the newborn's tiny nose, marveling at just how small she was. He'd had that same sense of wonder when holding Ava's new daughter. "It's amazing, isn't it?"

"Yes. I feel it every time I help with a delivery."

Clancy wasn't sure if that's all it was in this case. Maybe knowing how precarious the situation had been made him feel a little more exposed. A little more vulnerable. All he knew was that holding this little one felt right and good and—

"Is she okay?" Maria's anxious eyes were on them, reminding him this wasn't his baby or Hollee's, but someone else's.

He gave a forced smile. "She's doing great."

Hollee took the baby, laying her on Maria's chest, skin to skin, letting them bond.

The woman murmured to her newborn, stroking her fingers through the dark tufts of baby fine hair.

"I guess we'd better let the baby's father know she's okay."

Hollee laughed. "Oh, no! I totally forgot about him."

So had he.

When Clancy went through the door, he found the new dad sitting on a couch, head bowed low, hands dangling between his knees. His slumped posture said he expected the worst but had stayed put as he'd been told.

"Everyone's fine. You have a healthy baby girl."

His head came up. "A girl? I have a girl?"

Clancy nodded.

The dad came over and grasped Clancy's hand in both of his, shaking it wildly. "A girl! I have a baby girl!"

How would it feel to hear those words? That he had a daughter? His heart squeezed so hard it hurt, a wave of remorse crashing over him. He could have had that. If only his friendship to Jacob hadn't meant so much— if he hadn't been quite so ready to believe the worst about himself. And Hollee had married Jacob, so that kiss hadn't meant all that much to her. Except Clancy had turned his back on her, pushing her away before it ever really got started.

But why was he still dwelling on things that he had no damn control over?

"Congratulations." He nodded at the door to let the man know he could go in and be with his family. Hollee passed him in the doorway.

"I came to see if everything was okay."

"It is. I'm pretty sure the news I handed him was not what he expected to hear."

"I'm sure it wasn't." She sighed and rested her head on his arm for a second. "I wondered for a little while if we were going to be able to deliver good news at all."

"Me too." He liked the feel of her next to him, just like he'd reveled in holding that newborn a few seconds ago. Hollee's closeness made him wonder if she could sense the turmoil inside him. "They probably should go to the hospital to make sure everything is okay, but with how hard it was for us to make it here, I'm pretty sure they won't be able to."

"I agree. My only real worry at this point is swelling. We've had patients who've needed catheters for a day or two after some of those maneuvers."

He nodded. "I want to come back and check on her tomorrow."

"Not a bad idea." She sighed. "Is it weird to think that this baby and Randy are the best things we've done since coming here?"

Since he'd had the same thought, he shook his head. "No, I felt it too. But I'm sure all the patients we've seen the last two weeks have been appreciative." He knew they had. He'd heard thank-yous from almost everyone they'd treated, despite the long waiting times.

"They have. It's just that it's almost Christmas. And after seeing all the hardship Bender has gone through, today felt like a miracle. A pre-Christmas miracle. Working at a hospital, I sometimes lose sight of those kinds of things. I think I'd like to come back to Bender to help as they get back on their feet."

As someone who'd been on the other side of the equation, working in the field where he'd railed against the lack of modern conveniences that could have saved lives, he wasn't sure he necessarily liked practicing under less than ideal circumstances. But he did understand where she was coming from. There was somehow a sense of accomplishment and gratitude when you saved lives, even when things were far from certain.

When you worked your ass off and went the extra mile to make it happen.

"Field hospitals are not always what they're cracked up to be."

"You've already done all of this and more, haven't you?"

"The things I dealt with weren't pretty, neither did they produce something as beautiful as a healthy baby. But we did save lives."

Her eyes went to his scar. "You've seen horrific things."

It wasn't a question. "Yes, I have." He smiled. "But not today. Today was a good day."

"Yes, Clancy. It most definitely was."

The midwife came out, wiping her hands with a towel. "Good, I caught you. I hate to ask, but is there any way you could stick around until tomorrow?"

"We were already talking about coming back to check on things. I'm pretty sure there aren't any bed and breakfasts up here, though."

"Jerry—the father—actually has a little cabin out back that his mother lived in while she was alive. It's not much more than an efficiency apartment, but it does have a bedroom and a separate sleeper sofa in the living room. He asked if you'd be willing to stay there so someone is close. They only have two bedrooms and one has two other children in it." She smiled. "If there's not something crushing in town that needs to be taken care of, that is."

He glanced at Hollee, and she smiled. "I think that's a great idea."

The midwife blew out a long breath. "Thank you for everything. Gavin, their son, got through okay?"

"Yes, he did, and stayed in town so that Hollee could come with me. Let me call and make sure someone can keep him for the night. If so, yes, we'll stay."

"There are some canned goods in the pantry that should tide you over. I'm going to stay and sleep here on the couch. I can call if something happens."

"Please do." He gave her their cellphone numbers.

Now that it had been decided, Clancy's thoughts were straying back into areas they shouldn't be. Like the fact that he and Hollee would be alone in a cabin. Wasn't that the very thing he'd been thinking about earlier? About complications and possibilities?

Yes, but he'd better knock that last one right back out of his head. While he still could.

CHAPTER NINE

As they drove through the slushy backyard to get to the cabin, Clancy worked the controls on the handlebars of the ATV with the same dexterity he'd used to deliver that baby. He'd been sure and decisive, even as fear had tickled the back of her throat that they might not be able to pull it off. Despite her worries to the contrary, he really hadn't needed her help. He'd already been moving from one thing to the next in a logical order, climbing his way from simple to complicated.

Until he'd succeeded.

She had a feeling that succeeding was important to Clancy.

It was important to her as well, but there were things that mattered more. Like what they'd experienced today. That raw turbulence that made the human experience what it was. She wouldn't trade that for all the success in the world. Neither would she trade the rare vulnerability that she'd seen in Clancy after the baby had been born. He'd cooed to her and held her and had looked like he couldn't get enough of her.

Hollee had loved watching him with her. So much so that she'd had to take a step back so she didn't get caught up in his emotion. More than that, she hadn't wanted to disturb that sweet connection he'd had with that little one.

She snuggled against him for the last couple of yards, needing that connection with him herself, though she wasn't sure why. Maybe it was the aftermath of the struggle for life that made up the human experience. Even though in this instance she was going to pretend that it was caused by the bumps in the path between the houses.

They pulled to a stop in front of a cabin very much like the main house, only on a smaller scale. She got off the ATV and turned to look at him. "This is really cute."

"Cute." One of his brows hiked up. "You took the word right out of my mouth."

His lips curved in that crooked smile that she'd loved so much when she'd been in the throes of that high school crush. People who crossed his path today no doubt wondered if the smile was the product of his scars, due to nerve damage. But Hollee could assure them that his sideways grin was one hundred percent Clancy. He'd probably come out of the womb with that adorably quirky feature. At the thought of a group of nurses swooning over a baby Clancy, she laughed.

"What?" He glanced over at her, climbing off the vehicle and pulling the keys from the ignition.

"Nothing. Just wondering something." There was no way she was going to tell him what that was. It was far too dangerous to her psyche.

"You looked good, holding that baby," he said.

The change in subject made her smile. "So did you."

When she realized there was more to his statement than a simple observation, her smile faded. She'd asked herself that same question repeatedly. But there'd never been a ready answer.

She tried to tack more onto the last explanation she'd given him. "It was just never the right time, I guess. Jacob just…" She swallowed back the rush of emotions that were still raw and yet, oh, so familiar. Why hadn't he wanted a baby with her?

"Sorry, it's none of my business."

She could understand his curiosity, though. Her mom had often pestered her about the same thing, but it was pretty crushing to have to admit that you wanted a child when your husband had no interest in that at all. And by the end he'd barely wanted to sleep with her. She'd done the asking, and he'd evaded her. The insecurities she'd felt back then had been crushing and horrifying. In her worst moments she'd wondered if Jacob was cheating on her, or if he somehow knew about that kiss that she'd shared with Clancy. But unless Clancy had told him…

Which she very much doubted. After all, Clancy had backed away from her as well.

She licked her lips and decided to bare one wound. "I wanted them. But in the end Jacob…didn't."

"Oh, hell, Hollee, I'm sorry. Did he give a reason?"

"Just that he wasn't ready. And after five years of marriage I stopped asking. For anything." It felt good to finally say that out loud, even though Clancy probably wouldn't catch what she meant by that last part. A weight lifted from her shoulders.

His hand moved under hers, palm to palm. He didn't close his fingers around her, but his thumb did stroke across her skin in a way that sent a shiver through her.

She decided if he could ask a question, so could she. "You never got married."

"Nope. I never did." As if a window slammed shut, so did the shared confidences, his hand moving out from under hers.

Stung, she withdrew, her fingers twining together. So much for baring her soul. That door evidently didn't swing both ways.

As if realizing what he'd done, he glanced over at her. "I didn't mean that to sound harsh. I just never really met anyone I wanted to settle down with."

Evidently not. Maybe that was why he'd dated woman after woman, never quite finding what he'd been looking for. He'd added her to that list of not-quite-right rejects.

She blinked. Except they'd slept together a few weeks ago.

Ha! No sleep had been had by either party.

But there must still be some kind of attraction on his part, unless it was just old-fashioned lust between a man and a woman. Even she'd tried to pass it off as that but had wondered several times if that was exactly true. Their time together had stirred up feelings she'd thought were long sent to the ash heap. But when she blew on them, a vague glow appeared. Just the barest hint of something left over.

He rotated one of his shoulders as if trying to rid himself of something. "Let's go inside before it gets any colder."

Passing through the door ahead of him, she was surprised to see that someone had already started a fire in the woodstove in the main area. It must have been done while they'd been washing their hands and cleaning up. It was still chilly, but already warmer than it was outside. There was a stack of wood beside the stove that looked like it had been freshly dumped.

She walked over to the heat source, closing her eyes as she walked through a silky layer of warm air. In the background, she could hear Clancy talking on the phone to Matt, the FEMA liaison, telling him what their plans were and asking if there was someone who could take care of Gavin for the night. From the sound of it, that wouldn't be a problem.

That was good, because she was both keyed up and exhausted at the same time, each emotion warring for first place in her body.

So was something else, and it was making her feel slightly crazy. The waves of heat from the stove were starting to feel a little too good, were starting to remind her of other ways to stay warm. Like on the back of that ATV. Or twined together under the cozy weight of winter blankets.

Sex with him shouldn't have been as good as it was. But there she had it. A damn stove was reminding her how much she still wanted him.

"Are you okay?"

She blinked and mumbled that she was and started to move away from the fire, only to have him stop her with a look. He came to stand in front of her.

"What's wrong, Hollee? You've been acting weird ever since we walked through that door. Before that, even." Oh, Lord, had he guessed her thoughts?

"*I've* been acting weird? I could say the same about you."

"It's been a stressful week." He stared at her. "Are you sure you're okay with staying here with me? I can try to get you back to town and return on my own."

"I don't want to go back."

She left it at that, her teeth digging into her bottom lip. When Clancy followed the movement, her breath stalled. In his eyes was a familiar heat. Something much more than the tiny ember from their past.

"You drive me crazy sometimes. Did you know that?" His fingers touched her arm, trailed up it until he reached her nape.

"You used to tell me that all the time when we were younger." She was treading on dangerous ground, and she knew it. But did she care? Not at the moment.

"I'm not talking about that kind of crazy."

She already knew that. But, then, of course, he didn't know that he drove her insane either. That she'd been sitting here thinking crazy thoughts herself.

His thumb stroked the sensitive area behind her ear. "Do you want coffee?"

Coffee? The last thing she wanted was a hot beverage. What she wanted instead was a hot…

Oh, God. Something was seriously wrong with her.

"No. I don't want coffee."

He gave her that slow, devastating smile. "That's good, because I don't either. Do you want the bed…or the couch?"

This time when his hand moved, his thumb toyed with her bottom lip in a way that caused her whole body to sit up and take notice. God, if he was seriously asking her where she wanted to sleep instead of where she wanted to be with him, she was going to be horribly disappointed.

He leaned his forehead against hers. "Damn, Hollee, tell me we shouldn't do this. That we could get a call any minute saying we're needed in the house."

"A minute is all it would take for us to get dressed." She licked her lips. "And I can't say we shouldn't do this. Because it would be a lie."

He leaned back to look at her, and she wondered if she'd just made a fool out of herself. If he was going to clear his throat and warn her not to get too invested in him, that he was only passing through…

"Lying is a sin."

The way he'd said that… Lord, it was getting hot in here. "W-we wouldn't want to sin, would we?"

Putting his lips close to her ear, he whispered, "I don't know. I think it depends on which of the seven deadly ones we're talking about. Because I can think of one I might like to explore. At length."

Her heart leaped at the seductive edge to those words, and suddenly she was floating in the clouds even as she tried to chain herself to the nearest solid surface. Because she'd just been thinking about this, and it looked like she was about to get her wish, sin or no sin. Right here. Right now.

Clancy walked her backward until her back was against the first flat surface he could find, shrugging out of his coat as he went, not caring that his cellphone was still in the pocket. And when he covered her mouth with his, he swore he felt something shift inside him. Something besides the obvious, which was doing some shifting of its own at the thought of having her again.

And that tiny nudge that said he might want more than one night? Well, he wasn't going to stop and examine that too closely. Better just to enjoy the here and now and not look too far into the future.

But the idea of actually waking up next to her tomorrow morning?

That was a heady thought. A new shot of adrenaline burst onto the scene, bringing with it the same urgency he'd felt the last time he had been with her.

Spinning with her in his arms, he pushed her heavy jacket off her shoulders, letting it fall next to his. Then he leaned down and picked her up, carrying her to the room just behind the living room, where a bed covered with a simple cotton spread was waiting. "Drop or place?"

She laughed. "Surprise me."

His inclination was to watch her fall in a delicious heap on that bed, but since he didn't know how thick the mattress was, he decided to lower her gently instead, setting her in the exact center, head on the pillows. He followed her down, covering her body with his, loving the feel of clothing against clothing, knowing soon enough that was all going to change. But if he only had one night, he was going to take pleasure in the small things. In every second he had with her.

He slid one leg between hers, enjoying the way her softness cradled his body. Those curves and swells that seemed to welcome him home.

Home.

She was. Even as his mouth trailed up her neck and slid across her jawline, something tickled at the back of his thoughts. A little yellow light that signaled, *Caution! Judge your distance and choose well.* Hell, right now he wasn't going to judge anything. He was not going to wait for that red light—he was barreling right through this intersection no matter what the cost.

Hollee murmured something against his mouth, and he leaned back slightly to look at her. God, she was gorgeous, even as her eyes fluttered open and looked up at him with a slight questioning frown. He trailed an index finger down her nose. "It's okay. I just needed to see you. Do you know what you do to me?"

"Pretty sure." She wiggled against him. "If this is what I'm hoping it is."

"Oh, it is." He laughed. "It definitely is."

With that all the questions were done as he rolled over, taking her with him until she was sprawled on top of him. And when he pushed up into her, she bit his lip hard enough to make a shudder roll over him.

He wanted this woman with everything that he was. "Sit up, honey."

Doing as he asked, she straddled him, her legs pressed against the outsides of his thighs, giving a little wiggle. Hell.

"Like this?"

"Just like that." He reached up and slid his fingers through her hair, combing it back over her shoulders. "I want you to like this. Okay?"

"I promise I *will* like it." Her brows went up. "Okay?"

It was more than okay.

She leaned down and unbuttoned the

long-sleeved black shirt he'd put on for the ceremony earlier—why did that suddenly seem like ages ago?—tilting back when her fingers reached the spot where the buttons disappeared between her legs. The implication of her long pause made his mouth water. Then she went up on her knees and tugged his shirt free, so she could get at the rest of the buttons. When she settled back in place, she was centered on him in a way that shot a burst of hormones through his system.

And lust. That sin he'd mentioned a few minutes ago.

"God, Hollee."

She made slow circles with her hips, a knowing smile on her face as she watched him. Then her teeth clutched her lip as the movements changed, rocking back and forth and adding a bit more pressure. If she kept that up, they were not going to need the entire night. He reached for her, shoving her turtleneck up her torso, glorying in the way she lifted her arms to let him pull it over her head. Next came her bra, exposing more silky skin to his touch.

"Come here. I want to kiss you."

Hollee leaned forward, her breasts mashing against his chest in a way that made him take her mouth with a fierceness that surprised even him. She was heaven on earth. And she was all his. At least for tonight.

Her tongue licked across his lips, nipping at the corners, before she kissed him deeply once again. All the while her hips kept up that tormenting motion, making the fire that was already raging in his veins grow more intense by the minute. He did not want to ask her to get off him, but if he didn't he couldn't finish undressing her, and if he didn't finish undressing her...

He sat up, taking her with him, wrapping his arms around her back, his mouth still tight against hers. Finally he pulled back an inch or two. "Do you think you can stand up?"

"Possibly. My legs are a little questionable."

He chuckled. "Okay, then I'll do the standing."

Tipping her off to the side, she gave a squeal before laughing. "No fair."

"Nothing about this is fair." He stood, finding his own legs less than co-operative, but he somehow managed to shrug his shirt the rest of the way off, before divesting himself of his jeans and the remainder of his clothes. Then he undid Hollee's pants and tugged them down her legs, followed by her lacy undergarments. When he sat back down on the bed he was sheathed, his erection heavy and, oh, so ready.

Hollee must have sensed it as well, because in a flash she'd come around and straddled his hips again, her hands sliding up either side of his face. Her fingers feathered down his scars, her eyes following their track. Before he could frown, she touched her lips to the one on his cheek. "So sexy. So very you."

Then she rose up just enough to position him before coming down hard, the sudden squeezing heat that enveloped him taking his breath away. He curved his arms up her naked back, palms cupping her shoulders as she continued to take him inside her. The intimacy of her whole body sliding against his was something he would never forget. Never wanted to forget.

Her lips were at his ear, her breath warm and sexy, hissing out with each downward pump. One of his hands slid deep into her hair, bringing her face around until her lips were barely against his. He brushed over them again and again, the light contact contrasting with the full-on impact of what was happening below.

His tongue tingled with the urge to thrust into her mouth, but he held off, knowing once he did that it was all over. With one hand still in her hair, the other trailed down her back, coming to rest just above her butt. He pulled her in tighter, trying to up the contact point between them. It worked, because she moaned his name, her movements growing slightly erratic as he kept her pressed against him.

He could feel the building pressure, praying he could hold it off long enough for her to get what she needed. He angled his hips higher. Pushed harder.

Suddenly her knees clamped against his thighs, using the leverage to propel herself up. Then she shoved herself down and held tight, her body going off all around him in way that brought ecstasy. And need. In a second he'd flipped her on her back and rode her even as he poured himself into her in a rush that consumed every thought in his head.

His movements slowed, her legs wrapping around him as if afraid he was leaving.

Not a chance. There was nowhere he wanted to be other than here. With her.

Nowhere.

That thought spun round and round in his head like it was a centrifuge, separating out the feelings that were packaged inside that single word and whipping them away until only one emotion remained. The most important one of all.

Hell.

He loved her. She'd just incinerated all those layers of denial he'd been building over these last few weeks, until there was no longer any hiding from the truth.

Somewhere in the middle of that revelation he'd come to a stop, his body resting against hers, not sure what he was supposed to do with what he'd just realized.

Why did he have to do anything? They only had tomorrow and then they were headed back to Arlington. There was plenty of time to think about whether he should act on this. Or whether he should just let it fade away. Again.

And until then he was going to do exactly what he'd said he was going to do. Hold her until morning dawned and hope by then he'd come up with a plan that actually made sense. So he rolled off her and pulled her back against his chest.

"Mmm… Clancy?"

"Yes?" He loved how rumbly her voice was. Loved that it was because of what they'd just done.

"Can I sleep in your bed?"

He chuckled. "I thought it was your bed. I was planning on taking the couch."

A deep sigh rolled up from inside her. "I could argue this point, but I won't. So I'll just change the question. Will you sleep in *my* bed?"

He tucked her tighter against his hips. "Yes. I will, Hollee. Gladly."

She couldn't remember the number of times he'd woken her in the night. But his need for her had been heady. He was still sound asleep, and as much as she loved watching him, she could already see light coming through the thin shades. The sun was up. Since her phone wasn't nearby, she had no idea what time it actually was. Or if their hosts were waiting for them up at the house.

Or worse, if someone came knocking on the door…

"Clancy." She breathed his name right against his ear.

His eyes fluttered open. He looked at her with a slight frown. "You're here."

Something about that made her blink. Where had he thought she'd be? She'd asked him to stay with her.

Unless she was putting emphasis on the wrong word. Maybe it was the "you're" she should be focusing on. Surely he remembered who he was sleeping with.

Her insecurities about all the women Clancy had slept with when they'd been younger melded with Jacob's later rejections and she stood in a rush, her legs not quite ready to hold her. She braced them beneath her.

Clancy didn't form attachments. She'd learned that the hard way. Had she expected that to change, just because it was her in his bed rather than someone else?

"Hey." He held out a hand to her. "What is it?"

"Nothing."

"Didn't we already talk about lying?"

She gritted her teeth for a second. "It's light outside. We probably need to check on mom and baby." She found her clothes, pulling them on as fast as she could.

He sat up. "Slow down for a minute."

"You were right last night. We shouldn't have done this."

Reaching out, he grabbed her hand, stopping her frenetic movements. "Why not, exactly?"

Blinking hard, she decided to just lance the poison all at once and let it out. "I'm not like you. I can't just sleep with someone and then move on to the next person."

There was silence for what seemed like forever. "Meaning?"

She shook her head, feeling foolish somehow. So what if she wasn't as experienced as he was?

God, she knew exactly who he was, so why was she suddenly attacking him for this particular character trait? It wasn't like he'd tricked her into sleeping with him. No, it had been her choice. Wise or not. She needed to own it. But before she could say anything, Clancy beat her to it.

"I remember Jacob once saying something very similar to me. Going on and on about how different he was from me." A pulse worked in his temple, and he got up and gathered his clothes together. His mouth thinned, and he seemed to be warring with something. "I know you think the man you married was a real paragon of virtue—someone worthy of sainthood—but you might be surprised."

There was an ugly bitterness in his voice that shocked her.

"What's that supposed to mean?" Was he actually going to talk badly about someone who'd once been his best friend?

"I mean Jacob wasn't who you thought he was."

She swallowed, waiting for him to say the words that she'd somehow known in her heart but had never really been able to face. "He cheated on me, didn't he?"

He didn't say a word, just stood there like the damn stone that he was.

The world around her turned white for

a terrifying second before a wave of fury swept over her. "How could you keep something like that from me?"

He headed for the bathroom, but there was no way she was going to let him walk away from this.

She ran over and grabbed his arm, and he stopped but he didn't turn around. That's when she realized with startling clarity that he knew—*knew*—beyond a shadow of a doubt that what she'd suspected was true.

A question burned on her tongue like acid.

"Why do you think...?" She changed to different words. "*How* do you know?"

"I saw him. And he admitted it."

She let go of him, wrapping her arms around her midsection as wave after wave of hurt went through her. "And yet you said nothing. Just let him off without even a warning."

"You have no idea what I did or didn't do. But you're right about one thing. This was a mistake. One that won't happen again."

Before she could say anything else, he was through the bathroom door, shutting it behind him. Seconds later, she heard the sounds of the shower going.

She sank onto the bed, her thoughts swirling. Jacob had cheated on her.

And Clancy had known about it and had never seen fit to tell her. He'd just let her go on as if everything had been fine, when it hadn't been. He was supposed to have been her friend.

But evidently he had been Jacob's friend first.

So much for thinking her husband had simply not been ready for children. Had he and Clancy laughed about how gullible she was?

It all made so much sense now. Her horror grew until it was all-encompassing. She decided she wasn't going to wait for Clancy to get out of the bathroom. She was going to get her coat on and walk up to the house and see how mom and baby were doing.

And then, like it or not, she was going to have to ride back to town with him on that damned ATV. But that was the end.

She could either wallow in the past and rail against the present, or she could make a choice of her own: to finally move on with her life. Without Jacob or Clancy or the phantoms that would bang at her door whenever she saw him.

Maybe this had been about closure. She'd needed to know how the story turned out. And now she did.

Just like that, a long chapter in her life slammed shut.

As they headed back to town an hour later, Hollee only had one thought: she hoped like hell she was strong enough to leave it shut.

CHAPTER TEN

TWO WEEKS AND COUNTING, and it still hurt.

It was Christmas Eve. The artificial trees in the hospital foyer still blazed with lights and fake snowflakes still twirled from the ceiling, but the holiday had lost its luster somehow.

And she knew exactly the reason.

Clancy had disappeared from the hospital a few days after they'd got back. The official word was that he'd taken a little personal time. But rumor had it that he was rejoining the military. And yet Clancy's shadow was still here. In the hospital newsletter about the trip to Bender, in the pictures of him as Santa that still circulated around the hospital from time to time.

Whoever had said it was better to have loved and lost hadn't known what the hell they were talking about. Because if she'd insisted on going straight back to the compound after delivering that baby, instead of agreeing to sleep over, she might not even know what she was losing. But standing here today...

She knew. And it hurt so much she could barely breathe.

She and Kristen had had a sit-down talk, and her friend had vehemently disagreed with her for not going after Clancy. But how could she when he'd kept something so devastating from her?

When his life pattern was to walk away from anyone that might get too close?

He hadn't tried to contact her. She'd watched her phone for any signs that she'd missed a call. She hadn't.

She was just turning in the last of her paperwork for her shift when Ava appeared at the nurses' desk wearing an elf hat and long Christmas-tree earrings. Hollee smiled when she saw her, although her chest was tight.

Please, don't let her mention Clancy.

"You look festive."

"Thanks." Ava brushed one of the silver

earrings and sent the bells on the tree jingling. "I have to wear this stuff while I can. Christmas is almost over."

Yes, it was. And right now she was glad. "The baby?"

"She's fine. But Jen-Jen isn't who I came to talk about. Do you have a minute?"

Oh, Lord, this *was* about Clancy.

"I was just getting ready to leave, actually."

"It won't take long. And it's something you need to know."

A horrible thought hit her. "Is Clancy okay?"

"No. He's not."

Her lungs stalled. "Wh-what is it?"

Ava nodded toward the waiting room that was just down the hallway, setting those ridiculous earrings jingling. Once they got there, Hollee dropped into a chair, her heart clanging like a gong. "Ava, please, just tell me."

"I will, but I need to let you know about something else first. And I want you to know that I'm breaking a promise to Clancy in doing this."

"If he doesn't want you to tell me…"

"I have to. You'll see why in a minute. And I'm hoping it'll clear up a few things in the process."

This time Hollee didn't say anything, she just nodded for her to continue.

"It's about Jen-Jen's christening."

Maybe this didn't have anything to do with Clancy after all. "Please, don't feel pressured to invite me—"

Ava held up her hand. "Not only are you invited, but I want you to be her godmother."

Before she had a chance to digest that bit of information or respond to it, her friend continued.

"Jen-Jen's middle name is changing, though. I'm so sorry, Hollee. Clancy told me something that I didn't want to believe."

A chill washed through her, raising bumps along her arms. So he'd told Ava but not her? Wait, but Ava had been going to name the baby after Jacob, so she had to have found out recently.

"I think I know what you're going to say, and I already know. When did he tell you?"

"Just before Jen-Jen was discharged from the hospital."

"Before…" Which meant Ava had known

before she and Clancy had made love that first time. Before they'd left for Bender. And he'd still kept it from her, even as they'd been intimate.

"Clancy told me you didn't know. He made me promise not to say anything."

"I wish he hadn't. I can't believe he didn't try to contact me. Not once. All this time, I thought that Jacob was…" She shut her eyes. "I deserved to know. I felt like such a fool when I finally found out."

"Which probably explains why Clancy is suddenly so set on getting back into the army. Did you guys have a fight?"

"You could say that." She wasn't about to tell her that she and her brother had slept together. On more than one occasion.

Ava leaned forward and laid a hand on her arm. "Listen, Hollee, we can talk about Jen-Jen and all the other stuff later. I don't want to pry, but Clancy cares about you. Probably more than you realize."

Did it matter? He'd joked about lying being a sin when he'd been maintaining the biggest lie of all, allowing her to think Jacob was someone he wasn't.

She couldn't think of anything to say, and

maybe Ava took that as her cue to continue. "I am pretty sure he cared about you even before you and Jacob started dating. But I know my brother well enough to know that he wasn't going to step between you and his best friend. I think Jacob probably had a hand in that."

"You're wrong. Clancy dated pretty hot and heavy back then. He had a new girlfriend almost every week. He cared about me as a friend and that was it."

Ava stretched her legs out, crossing them at the ankles. The leggings she wore were also Christmas themed. "I remember his dating life suddenly going on hiatus for a few weeks before it picked up again. I'm pretty sure it was just before you went out with Jacob that first time."

Clancy had told her that kissing her had been a mistake. She'd been so hurt and angry, that when Jacob had asked her out, she'd accepted his invitation. The more she'd seen how easy it was for Clancy to slide in and out of relationships, the more she realized she did not want a man like that. And so what had started out as a revenge date had morphed into an "I want a man like this, and not that" manifesto. She'd convinced herself that she loved Jacob, but maybe she'd been in love with the idea of what he represented. Someone who'd been happy to remain monogamous. Only he hadn't been, according to Clancy.

"Does it matter?"

"Not to me. But someday it might to you." She uncrossed her legs and climbed to her feet, a batch of reindeer bracelets clanking together at her wrist. "I'm his sister. I know him. And I'm telling you, that man is hurting right now. And that's all I'm going to say on that matter. I just thought you should know."

"Thank you." She hugged her friend and then headed for the door. There was no sense in being angry with Ava. None of this had anything to do with her. But it did give her a lot to think about.

Had she been rash in walking out of that cabin before they'd finished talking? Possibly. But she wasn't sure what to do about it now.

Clancy had told her that kissing her had been a mistake ten years ago, and he'd told her the very same thing two weeks ago. And she'd believed him. Both times.

But what if he'd been lying?

Maybe she should be focusing on that rather than on his choices from a long time ago. She'd hurled a lot of hurtful words at him. Had she expected him to just stand there and take it, and then start whimpering about how sorry he was? No. That was not how that proud, bull-headed man's brain worked.

And she'd been pretty bull-headed herself.

So what was she going to do about it?

First thing, she was going to call the army and see if he actually had re-enlisted. And if she found him and he refused to listen to her?

The thought sent a river of regret streaming through her.

If he wouldn't, then she was going to have to accept that whatever had happened between her and Clancy was over and done with. And there was absolutely nothing she could do about it.

Hollee arrived in front of her house feeling like her mind was full of sludge, much like what that ATV had traversed that day in Bender. Only she wasn't up to wading through it right now.

The last shift at the hospital had been stressful and busy, and Ava's words had sent a spear through her heart. Right now she just wanted to crawl into bed with her dog. Only Tommie missed Gordy. She hadn't whined or barked, but she did sit in front of the door listening for any sounds. And when she did hear something, she cocked her head and inched closer, tail thumping on the floor in the entryway. But it was never Clancy and Gordy.

Putting her key in the lock, she went in and closed the door behind her.

Tommie wasn't there to greet her, which was odd. "Hey, girl," she called out. "I'm home."

Still nothing. A chill settled over her. Tommie was still fairly young, but with the problem she'd had with her eye, anything could have happened. Dropping her purse onto the entry table, she hurried into the living room, only to stop short.

A huge Christmas tree rested in the spot where Tommie's pillow normally sat. Okay, unless she was in the wrong house or hallucinating, that shouldn't be there. She hadn't put up a tree this year because of the trip. And when she'd arrived home she hadn't really been in a good place emotionally. So...

And then she looked closer and her mouth dropped open. The decorations on the tree looked eerily similar to the ones from Bender. But only the people who had been there knew about those. Was Kristen having a joke at her expense? Or trying to cheer her up? If so, it wasn't working.

"Kristen? Are you here?"

"She's not." A form stepped from behind the tree. "But I am."

"Clancy?" The buzzing of a million thoughts roved her brain, looking for some kind of logical explanation before settling on one thing. "Where are the dogs? And how did you get in?"

"Your mom, on both counts. They're staying the night with her."

"For the night. My mom...?" Her mother was in on whatever this was? Didn't she know that Hollee's heart was about to split in two? "I normally spend Christmas at their house."

"I know. Let's talk about that later, though. Will you come and sit with me?"

In a daze, she went to the couch and eased onto it, only to have Clancy sit right beside her. A small remote appeared in his hand and the tree suddenly lit up, its multicolored lights seeming to shift and change as the seconds ticked by in silence. Clear plastic strips dangled from the tree, just like the soda-bottle icicles one of the kids had made. And there was a garland…made of odds and ends of hardware.

She stared at it. "How…? Where…? That garland…"

"I made another trip to Bender two days ago. Randy's dad let me raid his found-items bucket, which is now a fifty-five-gallon drum, since everyone is eager to help him with the building project."

"You went there?" She turned to look at him. "But why?"

"I'll tell you, but first I need to apologize. For keeping the truth about Jacob from you."

"Even Ava knew." A new wave of hurt washed over her.

"Not until she chose Jay for Jen-Jen's middle name."

"You still should have told me. A long time ago. When I could have done something about it."

"I would have, if Jacob didn't come clean to you."

She frowned. "But he didn't."

"I know. He told me he would, but he didn't get the chance. His chopper crashed before he came off deployment." He turned to look at the tree. "And once I knew for certain he was dead, when should I have told you? While we were standing over his grave at the cemetery?"

She saw his point. "If Jacob had lived and refused to tell me—"

"I would have outed him. I told him I would, and he had no doubt that I would follow through."

Glancing back at the tree, she was amazed at how closely he'd replicated the one from Bender. And he'd done it all while she'd been at work.

Ava had told her something else, and she could only move forward if she knew the truth. "You kissed me once. A long time ago."

"I know."

"But then…all those girls. You couldn't change them out fast enough."

"I think you can probably guess why. Jacob told me he loved you and the last thing you needed was someone like me messing up your life. Well, he didn't say it in so many words, but I knew myself well enough to know it was true. Jacob was on the fast track to success, while I was too busy having fun and cutting every corner I could find. So before I got the chance to fulfill his prophesy… I bowed out." He shrugged. "Was it the right decision? I don't know. What I can tell you is that I am not the same person I was back then."

"So what you said about it being a mistake?" Suddenly all the pieces slid into place, and she knew Ava's timeline statement was right on the mark. And maybe Jacob had even known what had gone on between them. It had always seemed like such a coincidence that he'd asked her outright as Clancy had seemingly cast her aside. But she would never really know her late husband's motivation.

"That kiss *was* a mistake. But not for me. For you."

Her heart clutched inside her and she chose her next words carefully. "And all those girls?"

"A smokescreen. And, no, I haven't been on a date…a real date…in a couple of years." He put his hands on her shoulders and turned her toward him. "If Jacob had never convinced me of how wrong I was for you, and if I'd asked you out, what would you have said?"

She sensed this was important. Very important. "I would have said yes, Clancy. I was ready to say yes. But you never gave me that chance."

"I know that now."

The time to be angry about the past was over. She could either sit here and fume and push him away, or she could try to understand the thought processes of a very young man who had just been reaching adulthood. Wasn't there a wise man who'd said that the greatest show of love was when someone laid down his life for his friends? Clancy hadn't laid down his life, but he had sacrificed himself. For her. And from the way Ava had talked, it had been a pretty big sacrifice.

"The past belongs to the past, time to make a new beginning."

"What?"

"Just something someone once found in a fortune cookie." And something she needed to take to heart.

He was here to tell her something important. The tree was the key to it, since he'd taken the time to replicate it.

She touched his face and gestured toward the tree. "Tell me why you did this."

"I messed up ten years ago. I wanted to make sure I didn't mess up again." He captured her hand. "Those kids in Bender made a huge impact on me, especially Randy and his dad. The way he said he was going to rebuild that town using the items he'd collected from the rubble of the past. So this is me, letting these things symbolize our past and hopefully using them to build a future. *Our* future. I love you, Hollee."

Had he really just said that?

"Ava said you cared. But I didn't think... I heard you were rejoining the military."

"I almost did, and then I realized it would be one more mistake to add to my list."

She laughed. "We could have a debate

about who's made more of them, but now isn't the time."

"No, it's not."

"So you're not *in* the military?"

He squeezed her hand. "No. My commanding officer told me to go home and not to come back until I'd thought long and hard about it. So this is me, thinking long and hard."

Her eyes watered. "Then please don't go. Not this time."

Wrapping his arms around her, he pulled her against his chest. And the rightness of that was almost overwhelming. Hot tears splashed onto her cheeks, running into his shirt when she thought about all they'd lost. But more than that, about what they stood to gain by finally making things right.

"I was hoping you'd say that. I tried to show you with the tree, wanted it to be our starting point. As long as you love me back."

"I do. I realized I loved you when you gave your stethoscope to Randy. I may have even loved you ten years ago, but I was so young. Too young to really know my own heart."

He kissed her tears away and then slid

his arm around her shoulders. "I want this garland to grow. To come to represent our lives. Good moments and bad, with us adding something to it every year until we're both old and gray and this string stretches for miles with the things that make us...us."

He pulled a tiny box from his pocket, and Hollee clapped a hand over her mouth.

Snapping open the top, he revealed a ring, one that was very different from the ornate band Jacob had given her. Instead it was a ruby, her birthstone, set in a plain band of white gold. "I know it's not a traditional diamond but—"

"It's perfect, Clancy. So very perfect."

His eyes met hers, the brown irises glowing in a way she'd never seen before. "Does that mean you'll marry me and help me add to our Christmas tree? And maybe even our family tree?"

Family...

"You want to have..."

"Children? Yes."

Her eyes closed, and the joy that had been slowly expanding in her chest was eclipsed by a huge burst of love for this man. They'd both made mistakes, but she wasn't going to make one now. There was only one possible answer to his question. "Yes, Clancy. Oh, yes."

He kissed her, his mouth seeking, asking in a way that needed no words. And she answered him in the same way.

And when he got up from the couch and swung her into his arms, walking with purposeful strides toward the back of her house, she laughed. "I see we're wasting no time in this family endeavor."

"We're not. Because the dogs are at your mom's house, but they'll be back tomorrow morning. And if we have that little addition I mentioned earlier, this may be the only time we're truly alone for many, many years."

She took one last look at the tree with its garland and wound her arms around his neck. Maybe that tree would never come down. Maybe she would teach their children what it meant, so that they too would grow up with a sense of wonder, knowing anything was possible.

If they just loved hard enough to make it happen.

EPILOGUE

HOLLEE HELD OUT her arms for her new baby girl. Somehow it was fitting that she had been born on Christmas Eve. She and Clancy had just sat down to enjoy the falling snow with glasses of eggnog—his with rum, hers without—when she'd felt a sharp twinge. And then another. Soon they'd been coming with enough frequency that there was no ignoring them.

And Clancy, who was normally as solid as a rock, had done the cute New Dad Shuffle as he'd fumbled to grab her overnight bag and call Hollee's mom to ask her to check on the dogs. In between laughing at his impatience when she'd tried to catch snowflakes on her tongue and the care he'd taken with making sure she hadn't slipped on the way into the hospital, she'd watched him with a sense of wonder and love that only grew deeper each day.

Her parents and Clancy's mom hadn't been nearly as shocked by the news that they were getting married as she'd expected them to be. Instead, they'd celebrated with them, even when Hollee had insisted on having an intimate ceremony with a justice of the peace and close family only. Her first wedding had been a lavish affair that had felt wrong in so many ways. She'd grieved about not confronting Clancy about that kiss being a mistake when it had counted the most. But Clancy had told her to let it go, that they'd both done what they'd thought was right at the time. Love had won in the end, and that was all that mattered.

And it was a good lesson to teach their baby. Or babies. Clancy wanted one more, and since she'd thought she'd never have even one, she was thrilled.

And they would all make a pilgrimage to Bender, Virginia, as soon as they were able to. She wanted to visit Randy and help where she could.

Her husband perched on the side of the bed as the nurses cleared away the labor equipment. He leaned over and kissed her forehead. "Well, first Jen-Jen and now our Elissa Marie. My mom is getting two grandchildren in a little over a year."

"And my parents are getting their first. They're thrilled. Have you called them yet?"

"Right after I caught my breath, yes. But I asked everyone to wait about an hour before arriving en masse. I want you two all to myself for a little while. And you need to get some rest."

She reached up and touched his face, sliding her fingers over those beloved scars. She held off his frown by whispering, "They're sexy. And I love you."

"You're changing the subject."

"There'll be plenty of time to sleep. I'm so afraid I'll wake up and find out this is all a dream."

Just then Elissa let out a howl that threatened to take down the hospital.

Clancy laughed. "Definitely not a dream."

"Yes, it is. But as long as it's happening while I'm awake, it's okay."

Hollee had left the Christmas tree up all year and, true to what they'd said, they'd added their first piece to the garland, a hand-carved Santa to represent that day at the hospital when they'd both realized something special was happening between them. Clancy had actually insisted on having the picture of them from the newsletter framed, editing poor Kristen right out of the shot.

"Believe me, you are wide awake, sweetheart. And beautiful. I love you, Hollee."

"Love you too."

He leaned down, encompassing her and the baby in a hug that made her already mushy emotions even mushier.

She sighed, cradling her precious baby in her arms. "I'm so grateful, Clance. So very grateful."

"So am I."

Glancing out the hospital window, she saw the snow was still falling, the big fluffy flakes sticking to the glass and gathering on the sill. "It's almost Christmas."

"Yes, it is. Although I think Christmas arrived a few hours early. Elissa is the greatest gift I could possibly imagine."

She leaned her head against his arm. "Do you think Tommie and Gordy will accept her?"

"Are you kidding? They're going to love

her. I'm sure of it." He paused, and she could sense he wanted to say something.

"What?" A curl of fear went through her before she forced it away. There was nothing to be afraid of. Not anymore.

"Would it be okay, if a friend of mine came over to see the baby?"

"Of course. Who is it?"

"My commanding officer. The one who talked me out of re-enlisting and told me to stay and fight for what I wanted."

She smiled. "I'm glad he did. Because if not…"

"I'd like to think I would have eventually gotten there. He just gave me a push when I needed it most."

Wiggling back to the far edge of the bed, she nodded at the space next to her. "Lie down with me, Clance. Because you're right. I'm sleepy. But I promised myself I was never sleeping without you ever again."

Clancy took the baby and laid her carefully in her bassinet and then slid onto the narrow mattress beside his wife, draping his arm over her. "Sleep. I'll watch over you both."

So, with the promise that he would be

there when she woke up, she let herself relax against his lean frame. She was the luckiest girl on the planet.

As he tightened his arm around her she amended that thought. Make that two girls… they were the luckiest *two* girls on the planet. And she would make sure Clancy knew just how much he was loved.

This Christmas and every other.

* * * * *

*If you enjoyed this story, check out
these other great reads from
Tina Beckett*

A Family to Heal His Heart
The Surgeon's Surprise Baby
One Night to Change Their Lives
The Billionaire's Christmas Wish

All available now!